THE DUTCHMAN'S GIFT

Richard Baran

TotalRecall Publications, Inc.
1103 Middlecreek
Friendswood, Texas 77546
281-992-3131   281-482-5390 Fax
www.totalrecallpress.com

Copyright © 2015 by: Richard Baran
Edited by William R. "Will" Barshop

Copy Editors, Lisa Puck and Joseph "Bucky" Baran

www.buckbaran.com
All rights reserved

ISBN: : 978-1-59095-297-9
UPC: 6-43977-42979-0

Printed in the United States of America with simultaneous printings in Australia, Canada, and United Kingdom.

FIRST EDITION
1   2   3   4   5   6   7   8   9   10

To: A.M.D.G.

Author Richard Baran

holds a doctorate and two masters' degrees besides his bachelor's in business. A Navy veteran, he taught and coached for forty years at the secondary school and collegiate levels. His publishing credits include, a coaching text, *Coaching Football's Polypotent Offense"* a short story, *That Ain't No Walleye*, and several dozen articles in professional journals. Baran's first novel, *The Jacket,* was published by Total Recall Press as were his subsequent novels, *Where Have All The Go-Go's Gone, Part One and When Will They Ever Learn—Where Have All The Go-Go's Gone. Part Two.*

Dick and his eighth grade sweetheart, Carol, have twenty grandchildren and they divide their year between Franklin Park, Illinois; Phoenix, Arizona and Minocqua, Wisconsin.

Visit www.richardbaran.com for more information.

List of Characters

Riley "Rocky" Stone: Twelve year old boy from Chicago who experiences a life and death fantasy with an old miner in the Superstition Mountains of Arizona.

Warren "Rocky" Stone: Riley's grandfather who is retired and lives in Arizona. His new passion in life is hiking the mountains surrounding the Phoenix, Arizona valley and southwestern Native American history.

Jacob Waltz: The Dutchman and discoverer of The Lost Dutchman mine in the Superstition Mountains of Arizona. He befriends Riley Stone.

Mr. and Mrs. Stone: Riley's Parents

Elsa: Riley sister,

William and Emma: Riley's cousins who love to tease him.

Jesus and Guadalupe: Brother and sister who accidentally meet Riley in the Superstition Mountains. They are Riley's age and become his friends.

Blind Charlie: An old man who lives alone on a ranch near the Mexican border in Arizona. The Indians believe Charlie and his ranch to be cursed by evil spirits because Charlie is blind and lives alone on his ranch in the desert. He helps Riley escape an Indian attack.

About The Book

Riley "Rocky" Stone, a twelve year old boy on a family vacation in Arizona, finds what he believes is an Apache arrowhead while hiking with his grandfather and family in Arizona's Superstition Mountains. When Riley returns to his home in Chicago after the vacation he closely examines his arrowhead. He discovers that one side has etchings of three circles—two small and one large. His grandfather had explained to him that the Native Americans communicated with crude drawings using circles and stick figures; the circles representing stages of life; a figure drawn upside down meant death. When Riley rotates his arrowhead where the two smaller circles sit atop the larger circle he sees death replaced by a crude image of Mickey Mouse.

Riley's grandmother in Arizona notifies her family that she has won a trip for all of them to go to Disney World. Riley senses trouble and doesn't want to go. His father informs him that he has no choice. Once at Disney World, Riley has a desperate urge to ride the Thunder Mountain rollercoaster in the town of Tumbleweed. Before boarding the ride with his cousin, William, he tosses his arrowhead into what appears to be a well for drawing up water and makes a wish. During the ride through the darkened, twisting tunnels of Thunder Mountain, Riley experiences being tossed about in the rollercoaster's car. A violent surge seems to lift him out of the car. Before he realizes what has happened, he finds himself back in the Superstition Mountains on the same trail where he found his arrowhead. Only now he finds much more. The much more is an old bearded miner who identifies himself as Jacob Waltz. Jacob calls himself "Dutch" and he lives in the tunnels of a mine he has dynamited and dug out of the mountain.

While with "Dutch", Riley survives being attacked by three

renegade U. S. Cavalry soldiers who were AWOL from the Army. As Riley becomes more familiar with his new home in the mine, "Dutch" gives him a nugget as a souvenir. The odd colored chunk of stone barely fits in the palm of his hand. Riley, while exploring outside the mine with "Dutch" is away, meets a Mexican brother and sister who are about his age. They are part of a family of Mexican miners who are digging for gold and in search of Jacob Waltz's mine, "The Lost Dutchman" that is rumored to possess unheard of wealth. Riley and his two young friends survive an attempt on their lives by an Apache scouting party and flee to the location of the Mexican mining family on the Indian ponies. While heading for their family, Riley's two friends tell him of a rundown ranch belonging to a sightless old man named, "Blind Charlie" who is called Evil by the Indians. The Mexican miners attempt to hold Riley and have him take them back to the "Lost Dutchman Mine." Riley, with the help of his two friends, flees on horseback in the direction of the rundown ranch. A band of Apaches in search of their missing scouting party spot Riley on one of their ponies and give pursuit. With the help of "Blind Charlie," he finds temporary safety on the Evil ranch. The marauding band of Apache warriors ignores the evil curse and bad medicine attached to "Blind Charlie" and set fire to the ranch house with Riley and the old man inside. "Blind Charlie" acts as a decoy and helps Riley escape on his Indian pony. As Riley heads for the Mexican border with several Indians in pursuit, he finds himself back on the Thunder Mountain roller coaster at Disney World. He tells his story to his family and even shows them his souvenir nugget. No one believes him except his grandfather who knows the value of the nugget.

Lost Dutchman's Gold Mine

From Wikipedia, the free encyclopedia by Chris C. Jones
www.wikipedia.org/wiki/Lost_Dutchman's_Gold_Mine

In many versions of the story, Weaver's Needle is a prominent landmark for locating the lost mine.

The **Lost Dutchman's Gold Mine** (also known by many similar names) is, according to legend, a very rich gold mine hidden in the southwestern United States. The location is generally believed to be in the Superstition Mountains, near Apache Junction, east of Phoenix, Arizona. There are also theories that the mine lies a considerable distance beyond the Superstition Mountains, in Mexico. There have been many opinions about how to find the mine, and each year people search for the mine. Some have died on the search.

The mine is named after the German immigrant Jacob Waltz (c. 1810–1891), who purportedly discovered it in the 19th century and kept its location a secret. ("Dutchman" was a common American term for "German", as seen in the term Pennsylvania Dutch, derived from the German word for German, "Deutsch".)

The Lost Dutchman's is perhaps the most famous lost mine in American history. Arizona place-name expert Byrd Granger notes that, as of 1977, the Lost Dutchman's story had been printed or cited at least six times more often than two other fairly well-known tales, the story of Captain Kidd's lost treasure, and the story of the Lost Pegleg mine in California. Robert Blair notes that people have been seeking the Lost Dutchman's mine since at least 1892,[1] while Granger writes that according to one estimate, 8,000 people annually made some effort to locate the Lost Dutchman's mine.[2] Former Arizona Attorney General Bob Corbin is among those who have looked for the mine.[3] Others have argued the existence of the mine has little or no basis in fact. But as noted below, Blair argues that all the main components of the story have at least some basis in fact.

According to many versions of the tale, the mine is either cursed, or protected by enigmatic guardians who wish to keep the mine's location a secret.

Chapter 1

"Kind of looks like an arrowhead to me, Rocky," his grandfather said to Riley, as they stood face to face on the pebble strewn trail that barely resembled a faint path. If someone looked hard and long enough and used their imagination there was a path.

Rocky was Riley's nickname. His grandfather had dubbed him with the name because Riley preferred crawling on the ground from the moment his mother first took him outside and set him down. "You think so, Grandpa," said Riley holding up the triangular shaped, jagged thin rock in the palm of his hand and glancing up at his grandfather. He couldn't see his eyes. They were hidden behind the aviator style sunglasses he always wore. All of his grandfather's glasses made him look like the pilot of some jumbo jet liner. He couldn't see much of his grandfather's face either, the top half protected from the broiling sun by a black, genuine Stetson hat that resembled something worn by a weather-beaten, battered cowboy. "You think, Grandpa?" he asked politely. He was always in awe when he talked to his grandfather even though conversations didn't come that often.

"Could be Apache," his grandfather said. "They've roamed these Superstition Mountains for a couple hundred or so years."

"You think?" the young grandson asked again.

"I think, Riley," his grandfather, Warren said, sensing it was time to head back to the main trail. The trail was marked by small piles or short stacks of rocks called cairns; the markers spread out and spaced generally where there was evidence of a trail splitting off in two directions. His grandfather had hiked for almost fifteen years after retiring to Arizona. He had sold his meat packing business in Chicago and took to the mountains and foothills as if he were a native Arizonan or, at the very least, a member of one of many Native American tribes indigenous to the southwest.

Warren "Rocky" Stone, Senior loved the Arizona mountains; loved being on a trail surrounded by nature that was one hundred and eighty degrees different than his beloved Wisconsin and the Northwoods where he had spend most of his life fishing Walleye and Musky. In the mountains, the elder Stone could purge his mind of loading docks, slaughtered animals turned into ethnic sausage products and unmerciful Chicago weather trying to dress itself as the four seasons. He learned to respect the Sonoran Desert trails and the mountains from day one. Staying alert to time, mentally marking his location and keeping hydrated were keys to getting off a mountain trail in one piece. The cairns would guide them back to Riley's grandmother, parents and his sister, Elsa. "Time we start down the mountain to the trail head," he said nonchalantly. "We don't want to be stuck up here at night, not with bobcats, coyotes, a hungry cougar, diamondback rattlers and a pack or two of wild donkeys."

"Really," said Riley, his eyes bigger than the arrowhead still clutched in his hand.

His grandfather gave a nod and said, "Lead the way,

Rocky." He preferred using his grandson's nickname that was the same as his, the name tagged on him when he played football at Weber High School in Chicago as a bruising fullback.

The arrowhead stayed clutched in Riley's hand during the long ride home from the hike as the rented van carrying the family sped west on the 101 Loop to Peoria where his grandparents lived in a retirement community. On the last day of their vacation, the arrowhead never left Riley's hand. He had awaked to find the arrowhead poking him in his nose. During the ride to Sky Harbor and the flight home to O'Hare, Riley and the arrowhead were one. They stayed that way as the family was being driven home, courtesy of his Uncle Joey, his dad's brother, to the octagon brick bungalow where the Stone family lived across the street from ShabbonaPark on Chicago's north-west side.

"It's an honest to God Apache arrowhead," he said, to his older cousin, William, after his mother had finished talking to her sister, his Aunt Kit on the phone. "Grandpa Warren swore on a stack of Bibles that it was," he said into the phone. "Did you ever hear of Geronimo and Cochise?"

"Yeah, I head of 'em," said William, his voice sounding as if he didn't care while trying to hide his envy from his younger cousin. "So what's the big deal?"

"The big deal, Mister Hot-shot High School Freshie is that our grandfather said it could have belonged to them," said Riley, his head seeming to bounce up and down with excitement as if he were a toy bobble head doll. "That's what he said, William. It's an Apache arrowhead and I found the thing under some dumb rock I kicked over." He laughed, "I almost broke my stupid neck when I tripped and landed on my hands and knees. That dumb arrowhead almost got shoved up my nose. " He couldn't contain his excitement and finally said, "I'll show it to you and Emma when you guys come over with your mom and dad to see the pictures of Grandma and Grandpa's retirement house in Arizona."

There was no way Riley could sleep that first night back home after the family vacation to Arizona. "Time for bed," his mother had said to Riley and his sister, Elsa.

"Ah, Ma, do I have to?" moaned Riley. His moan didn't have a chance to go any further.

"Get your butt in bed," ordered his father.

Riley kicked at the covers all night. Then there were times when he thought his heart was going to explode. He tossed. He turned. Then he tossed and turned some more until his bed covers were wrapped around his neck and he thought he was being choked to death by a giant Blue Snake, one of many species of snakes his grandfather had told him about. Finally, he reached over and turned on the Bears helmet lamp that was on his night stand. For the first time since he and his family returned from Arizona he had a chance to examine the arrowhead. He spit on the stone, rubbed the moisture around the rough surface and then dried and polished it with the corner of his bed sheet. He put it under his lamp, examined it hoping to find some mysterious secret. He didn't. At least that side didn't have a message from some ancient warrior or Apache chief directing him to the famous Lost Dutchman mine his grandfather had told him about as they walked down the mountain.

Riley let loose with another drop of spit and started up his polishing and buffing routine on the arrowhead's other side and that's when he saw it. The scratched outline didn't make sense. "Apache," he muttered not knowing what to make of the unintelligible design looking back at him. He wasn't the smartest kid in school, but he knew what a circle was from his math class and very brief introduction to basic geometry. His grandfather had explained concentric circles to him, calling them rings; even adjacent circles were mentioned when describing the series of crude figures etched in a rock face that they had discovered while hiking. The circles and stick figures looked like something he would have drawn on his Big Chief tablet with a number two lead pencil when he was in kindergarten. His grandfather had enhanced his grandson's knowledge of the ancient circles and figures drawn by Native American people. "Rocky," his grandfather started to explain, "that's the way people communicated way back when. Their picture engravings tell us about their history. Those rock carvings were the way they wrote."

"Cool, Grandpa," replied Riley ready to soak up every word his grandfather said to him. "And, simple things like some circles say things?"

"Yep," said his grandfather. "There can be one to four rings, Rocky," he said, sounding as if he had Native American blood in his veins. "They describe life from birth to death. Depending on the ring or hoops, they can mean things like bless, heal and protect."

Strange sensations tingled through him. It was as if his

cousin William was shaking his hand with a hidden joy buzzer, the vibration shooting through his hand and up his arm, scaring the daylights out of him. He sat up and kicked is legs over the side of his bed. Bending forward he leaned toward the light and held the arrowhead under the shade. Nothing showed up. Then he realized he hadn't checked the side he had just cleaned. He turned the arrowhead over and held it close to the light. That's when he saw it. The reflection of what looked like a circle bounced off the shinny Bears helmet. The navy blue helmet didn't' make the markings on the arrowhead very clear, but it did show Riley that the circles he saw could be an ancient Apache symbol; maybe more. He had a magnifying glass somewhere in his room. He used it mainly to turn the sun's rays into hot pinpoints trying to start a piece of scrap paper or cardboard on fire. "I don't know Apache," he muttered, his frustration level growing, "But, I'm going to find out." He was out of bed and opened his closet door to be greeted by a mound of his clothes, athletic gear, scattered school books and several Oreo cookie wrappers. Most important there was a book he got a year ago at Christmas about Native Americans and their symbols, carvings and petroglyphs. Magnifying glass in one hand and the arrowhead in the other, he held it up to the closet light. There was a large circle with two smaller circles underneath and attached to the larger one. "What the heck is that?" he asked his closet.

He turned the arrowhead over until the two smaller circles were on top of the larger one. Then he turned the arrowhead back to where the two smaller circles were under the larger one. His grandfather's explanations of circles and figures were vivid. One in particular stood out and he wondered asking silently,

"Am I looking at the top or the bottom?" He could hear his grandfather explain to him: "Rocky, if the Indians drew a figure upside down, it meant death."

Riley's next glance at the arrowhead had him wondering. "Death," he thought, as his cherished arrowhead was quickly losing his interest. "Why would some Indian want me dead?" he asked his bedroom. "I wasn't even born back then. What did I do to hurt them?" Riley thought for a moment then began feeling more secure. "Heck," he muttered, "that was then and this is now. There aren't no bows and arrows around for some warrior to use on me." He felt better and rotated the arrowhead so the two smaller circles were now on top of the larger circle. That's when Riley "Rocky" Stone's knees almost gave way.

Chapter 2

Riley knew all about being scared. So he thought. His cousins would sneak up on him unsuspecting, grab his arms or pinch his butt and shout, "Boo!" or some other unintelligible screaming yell designed to make a person jump. William was the best, but his friends from St. Pricilla's were a close second. This time, however, scared took on a whole new dimension. He couldn't go back to bed because sleeping was out of the question; not with what he saw or thought he saw after he accidentally dropped the arrowhead that felt on fire. The arrowhead sat looking up at him from the mound of his belongings on the closet floor challenging him, saying, "Okay, Rocky, just how brave are you? Brave enough to be an Apache warrior. Brave enough to find the Lost Dutchman? Brave enough to take on the Superstition Mountains?"

Riley found himself sweating, his hands trembling. The Saturday morning light worked its way through his bedroom window curtains, the ones covered with all kinds of balls from different sporting events. He spied the Oreo wrappers around the arrowhead and felt as if he hadn't eaten for a week. In an instant he picked up his arrowhead, turned off the closet light and was down the stairs from his converted bedroom in the attic of their house and on his way to the kitchen. When he heard his name he had almost shot straight up as if launched from the mini-tramp in their back yard when he heard his name. The only reflex that mattered to him was that his arrowhead stayed clutched in his hand.

"Riley," his mother repeated. "Are you feeling okay?"

Even knowing it was his mother talking couldn't keep him from turning ashen. "I'm fine, Mom," he stammered.

"You don't look fine," she said. Then turning to Riley's father who sat at the rectangular light pine kitchen table she said, "He doesn't look fine, does he JR?"

"Ah, he looks okay," his father said. "Probably suffering from jet lag and worn out from being drug all over the Sonoran Desert by my screwball father, the reincarnation of Grizzly Adams." His father's head went slowly from side to side several times. "My father is the ultimate piece of work. I'm still at a loss as to how my mother managed to stay with him all of these years."

"I sure hope he's not coming down with that awful Valley Fever," his mother replied. The palm of her hand went to Riley's forehead. "Do you have a fever?" she asked, her hand traveling down to one cheek and then the other.

"I'm fine, Mom," he said.

"Why are you up so early?" his father asked. "Usually we have to dynamite you out of bed."

"I couldn't sleep," he said, taking a half gallon carton of milk from the refrigerator and pulling a chair away from the kitchen table. "Maybe you were right, Mom. Maybe I have that jet lag thing you talked about." He wanted to tell his parents what he saw etched into one side of his arrowhead, but he feared they wouldn't believe him. Worse yet, his mother would probably make him throw the arrowhead in the trash or the recycle bin. She was always warning him about his room being filled with clutter. He could feel the arrowhead in his pocket. There was no way he was going toss out the Apache treasure he had found on the trail he had hiked with his grandfather up on the Superstition Mountains.

"Well," his father started with a big smile, that was uncharacteristic of him. A quick upturn at the corners of his mouth meant uproarious to his father who walked around most times with a bored look on his face. "Guess where this here Stone family is going in little over a month once school gets out?" He didn't give his son a chance to answer. "Your Grandpa and Grandma Stone in Arizona are treating all of us, your two cousins and your aunt and uncle, to a trip to Disney World."

The milk carton slipped from Riley's hand and he caught it just before it had a chance to land in his lap. "Disney World," he repeated fighting the urge to run back to his room and hide under his bed. He didn't hear a word of explanation coming from his father; never noticed his mother's enthusiasm about being told of the trip by her in-laws. It was an early Christmas present. Riley's grandmother had won the grand prize in a contest that she had entered. His grandmother was always entering contests or trying to be the seventh caller or entering the Publisher's Clearing House Sweepstakes without buying any magazines. Once a month, it seemed, she would call her daughter-in-law, Riley's mother, telling her the good news about winning dinner for two or a pair of tickets to something. She had won a flat screen television; there were two free golf lessons where she left after one and a half because the golf store wanted to sell her a three hundred dollar driver that would elevate her game to where she could possibly compete on the LPGA tour. His grandmother was lucky she could even hit a golf ball. Hitting it long and straight, even down the middle of the fairway, was impossible.

"Grandma really won a trip like that?" asked Riley, not surprised that she had, but more astonished at her string of luck. At least six to eight times a year his grandmother would call the house, her "hello" starting out with, "Guess what I won?"

Riley's father could never get over his mother's luck. "I've never won a single thing in my entire life," he would carp. "That mother of mine must wear a necklace of four leaf clovers and have rabbit feet earrings." He'd pause after his stock comment, think about what he would say next and then say it, the same comment all the time. "She must have a lucky horseshoe up her backside."

Riley's mother would admonish his father, sigh and add. "I guess you're right. I just wish I had her luck."

Riley's father let out a laugh "Why do you need her luck?" he asked. "She just gave you the grand prize. Eight of us are going to Disney World. All we've got to do is keep the kids fed and us adults ever mindful of cocktail hour."

What shook up Riley before he heard about the family vacation to Orlando, Florida was the fact engraving of what he was sure was Mickey Mouse on his arrowhead. He would probably had never noticed it if he hadn't rotated his prize find.

At first glance, upside down, all he saw was a big circle with two tiny circles underneath looking like tiny legs supporting the big circle. He blinked thinking he would see two dots and a curving smile representing a Happy Face. There wasn't a face, happy or sad. He gave his treasure a slow turn until the tiny legs took on a new meaning. "Gee," he whispered. "I don't believe it." He paused, caught his breath and gave the arrowhead a turn into its original position. "Looks like a crystal ball with round feet," he said. The arrowhead got another slow turn until the feet no longer looked like feet. "It can't be," he muttered fighting the urge to run down the stairs to the bathroom. "It can't be."

Riley studied the arrowhead and the almost perfect trio of circles. "William's never gonna believe this. He ain't never gonna believe it," he said, with a sigh. "Oh, man, he's gonna laugh his butt off at me. Laugh his butt off!"

The arrowhead felt warm in Riley's hand; at the same time it was almost pushing against his palm as if trying to get his attention; to tell him something. That something was what Riley didn't want to know. "We're goin' to Disney World," he said. His head went from side to side. "No way am I goin'," he muttered. "Home alone, baby. If some kid in a movie can stay home all by himself during Christmas, I can stay here for a whole week during the summer."

After his knees had stopped shaking and the fear of being

laughed at or questioned by his whole family, aunts, uncles and cousins included, Riley went to his desk and turned on his computer. He could hear his grandfather's words up on the Superstition Mountain trail where they had hiked several days earlier. His grandfather's words had him searching the Internet for the Lost Dutchman Mine. He quickly found it and much more. Tales, magic, mystery and even death came up on the screen. There was a picture of Weaver's Needle, the upward stalk of jagged rock rumored to be the location of the Lost Dutchman. His computer mouse kept sliding, skimming, prodding and searching. There was the history of the mine, the mention of a man named Jacob Waltz, a German immigrant who shot at and even killed those who followed him to find his mine. "He killed people," said Riley aloud. "Gee, that Jacob guy must've been some kind of a crazy man."

Riley's right hand moved the mouse more deliberate by now, the cursor stopping on the legends and the myths attached to the mine. "Grandpa sure didn't dump a load of crap on me," he said, as details of the Apache went down his computer screen. Then soldiers from the U.S. Cavalry galloped across his screen. "Probably greedy deserters," his grandfather had said to Riley when he mentioned who he called, Horse Soldiers. The Internet made mention of a Mexican family, the Peralta's, who were rumored to have worked the mine sending the gold they found back to nearby Mexico. Then the Apaches or the Cavalry found them. Maybe a mysterious sniper his grandfather had mentioned found them. "Story has it," his grandfather had started out by saying, "many of them Peralta folks ended up dead." His grandfather paused and looked at Riley over the tops of his sunglasses. "Don't know how many lived or how many didn't, but the historical folks make mention that some blood might have been spilled. His grandfather had ended his story of the Lost Dutchman with a combined question and quick answer. "Rocky, do you know what you end up with when you turn greedy?" His answer came in a split second. "Nothin'," he said, his head going up and down before adding, "Maybe even dead."

Chapter 3

Riley did express his desires about not wanting to go to Disney World. He had intentionally left out his fear that something bad would happen to him. That something bad was in the form of three faint circles etched on one side of his arrowhead.

Regardless of how he felt, he was now well on his way sitting in an aisle seat next to his mother and sister. Elsa got the window seat; his mother leaning next to her so she could also get a chance to look at the scenery below. All they saw were clouds for most of the flight. He saw his father seated across the aisle from him. The elder Stone dozed off in between bouts with a crossword puzzle, his head rolling back and forth on the head rest. Riley tried to sleep, but his arrowhead in his right pants pocket wouldn't let him. It seemed to be trying to burn a hole in his leg each time his eyes got heavy. "Aw, Ma," he thought. "Why didn't you let me stay home?"

Riley had given his best acting effort of all time to try to get out of the trip. The camera on him, he emoted his rehearsed lines to his mother. His voice sounded hoarse and his eyes drooped like a mutt standing disappointed next to an empty garbage can in a Chicago alley as he said to her, "I'm too sick to go to Disney, Mom." A cough followed his announcement. "I'd probably up-chuck on the way to the airport." There were two more short coughs followed by his fists gouging at his eyes and he added, sounding as if he were placing a death sentence on himself, "You guys go without me. I'll be okay."

"It's definitely the Valley Fever," his mother had informed the entire family, her in-laws in Arizona included.

As Riley continued to give his Academy Award winning performance and making his supreme sacrifice for the good of his family, his mother was reprimanding her father-in-law. Harsh words, for her, were being uttered into her cell phone. "You could've at least told us that your grandchildren's health, even their lives, would be at risk walking around in that godforsaken, silly Superstition Mountain of yours."

Riley could sense that the person at the other end of the phone made a comment that didn't agree with his mother's scientific medical findings. She had pulled the phone several inches away from her ear, glanced at it in disbelief, before returning it several seconds later and stating: "Well, that's what I read in People and they should know." The phone moved even farther from her ear.

There was no valley fever, only what had now become the curse of Superstition Mountain. That curse, and the connection of an ancient Apache arrowhead with the symbol of Mickey Mouse etched into the stone, had Riley feeling a sense of foreboding the moment he made the connection between the Lost Dutchman mine and his arrowhead with the three faded circles. He sensed something was going to happen to him and that the something wasn't good even if Mickey Mouse was involved.

"Riley," his dad said, trying to reassure his son as they waited in line to board the plane, "the trip will be fun. "You'll have a ball at Disney World. You and your cousins will be so worn out from going on all the rides so many times that none of you will complain about having to go to bed." His tiny smile formed. "So, get well real quick," he said. "We'll be in Orlando in a few short hours."

Riley almost tore the arm rests from his seat when the plane touched down. He had dozed off just after the flight attendant had made the seat belt announcement. He was worn out. His melodramatic performance depicting critical illness had taken its toll on him. Then being caught in a cross-fire between his mother and father with his aunt and uncle contributed to his agony with comments like: "Nephew, do you have rocks in your head?" That shot came from his uncle. His aunt was more subtle saying, "Florida sunshine, fresh air, orange juice and all of us there to take care of you will make a wonderful vacation for all of us." His cousin, William whispered to him, "What's eatin' on your butt, Dorkus?" William's sister, Emma said even less stating: "You Sick-o." Riley's sister, Elsa never said a word, walking backwards through the boarding gate at the airport looking at her brother and holding up her thumb and forefinger in the shape of an L and keeping it pasted to her forehead.

Grandma Stone's Grand Prize didn't include lodging within the Magic Kingdom, but the hotel was close by. Riley's father and uncle rented a van for both families to get around. There wasn't much getting around once the van was in the Disney parking area. A busy day quickly extended into a night filled with lights and fireworks at Disney World. As Riley's father had predicted, all of them were worn out from the trek through airports, the lines, a car rental, unpacking at the hotel and then to the Magic Kingdom itself.

After his first full day, Riley appeared to be a vision of health. Gone were the sporadic coughs smothered in groans and the Pluto sad eyes.   His arrowhead never saw the Florida sunshine the first day.   It was forgotten in the pocket of his khaki shorts. The next morning was different. He transferred the arrowhead to the pocket of his favorite pair of hiking shorts. He had his hiking boots on with the laces double knotted the way his grandfather had taught him, his simple lesson ending with: "That way you won't trip on a shoe lace and fall off the mountain."

Both families piled in the van after what resembled breakfast. Both his mother and aunt had sung out together like a cheap commercial in reply to an assortment of complaints: "Energy bars are healthy. Energy bars are good for you."

"Is this all we get?" the quartet of children in the midst of growth spurts had asked.

"We'll eat in the park," Riley's uncle had said. All of the kids knew that eating meant more healthy energy bars smuggled in oversize purses and a giant duffle bag. "Burgers on the grill tonight," announced Riley's father. "I'm cookin'."

"Tell your old man I'm starvin' now," said William.

"You ain't the only one," said Riley, his voice a whisper.

Riley sensed it the moment he set foot inside the park. Actually, he felt the eerie sensation the moment he looked at the brochure and saw the picture. The caption called it Big Thunder Mountain. It sprouted out behind a mining town, In front was the picture of what was supposed to be a run-a-way locomotive, a miniature version leading a series of mining cars filled with tourists. It was billed at a wild roller coaster ride. Riley didn't care. His eyes were glued to the picture and the mountain in the background. Disney may have called it Big Thunder, but he knew it as part of the Superstitions, a prominent landmark called Weaver's Needle. Gold prospectors and those searching for the Lost Dutchman mine for years and years were convinced that the Needle marked the location of the mother lode. His grandfather had emphasized that well known fact several times when they hiked together.

Before anyone could put the day's itinerary into place, Riley shouted out, "Wow, this Thunder Mountain roller coaster thingy looks awesome. Can we go on it first before the lines get too long? Can we?" He waved the brochure under the noses of his sister and cousins. "This looks sweet!"

Without getting an answer or permission from his parents and not waiting for his sister and cousins, Riley was off in the direction of Big Thunder Mountain.

Chapter 4

Riley shuffled nervously off to the side of where the line had formed for Big Thunder Mountain. He beat his family by several hundred yards and couldn't believe what he was seeing and feeling. His Apache arrowhead felt on fire in his pocket, his hand barely able to touch it. He was an excitable kid by nature, but now he felt as if he were about to jump out of his skin. His family caught up to him and he quickly took a place in line ushering them into queuing up for the ride.

"This looks stupid," William said. "Who ever heard of a town called Tumbleweed? Sounds like something you'd read about in one of your comic books."

"It looks kind of cute and something your uncle and I might enjoy," his aunt said, inching forward in line and overwhelmed with the scenic details of what was depicted as an abandoned mining town.

"Getting hotter," his father muttered. "I can feel the humidity already. I hate humidity."

"Oh, the weather's beautiful, JR," Riley heard his mother say. "Stop complaining and enjoy the gift your mother sent."

The line seemed to leap forward until the Stone family was inside the abandoned and haunted mining town of Tumbleweed. Riley didn't have to read about a supernatural force that the brochure said dwelled within the mountain he could see beyond the Big Thunder Mountain railroad station where the rollercoaster awaited. As they moved ahead, careful to stay in their group of eight, Riley saw what he thought was a wishing well off to the side situated among abandoned crates, barrels and boxes. On one of the boxes was stenciled with the faded word, Dynamite. His arrowhead seemed to be scorching his leg as his family positioned themselves alongside the roller coaster, its cars looking like they had just been pushed out of a mine. Before he knew what he was doing, he tossed his Apache arrowhead into what he saw was a well for water thinking it was a wishing well. It could've been a rain barrel or a barrel once attached to the back of a Conestoga wagon holding precious drinking water for the settlers creeping and bouncing across the rock and sand of desert. Riley's excitement and new found curiosity pulled him into the car, the safety bar securing him in his seat next to William.

"I still think this is stupid," muttered William. He and Riley were in the last seat of the last car. "I don't hear no stinkin' thunder coming out of that mountain," he said as the roller coaster started forward. The sound of steel wheels against steel rails mingled with the scattered applause and subdued cries of excitement from the other riders. A series of turns, minor dips and slight climbs later, Riley found himself entering a tunnel. His head swiveled back and forth as he tried to get used to the darkness. He couldn't see a thing! His inside leg, the one that was next to William, moved toward his cousin as the car turned with a jolt, but he didn't feel another leg. He didn't feel a thing! There was another jolt, the car going into a dive that was followed by a quick turn left, another turn left and then a jarring turn right. That's when he found himself on all fours looking down at what resembled the trail where he had found his Apache arrowhead. There was no arrowhead with three etched circles staring at him this time; only a pair of dusty worn cowboy boots.

Chapter 5

Trepidation and downright fear joined forces to grab Riley. His eyes had no problem adjusting to his new environment. Wherever he was, he found himself kneeling on all fours. Black had gone to bright and he squinted, his blurred, distorted stare reluctantly inching up. He got as far as the waist of a tattered pair of dirty, heavy brown pants held up by wide red suspenders; the pants looked older and about as tortured as the boots he first saw. A calloused right hand with part of the little finger missing, emerged from his blurred, distorted view and was being offered to help him get up off the ground.

"That was quite a landing, Junge," said a voice sounding as if it had crawled from the gravel covered floor of a mine; the statement coated in a strange accent, the hand still being offered.

Riley's head tilted back as far as he could move it. The angle of the sun made it difficult for him to make out the stranger's face. At first he thought his grandfather was offering him help just like he always did in his subtle standoffish way. Grandpa Stone was always there for him, especially before he and his grandmother surprised the family by moving to Arizona. He remembered to the letter what his grandfather had said to Riley's father when answering the universal question: "Why are you and Mom moving?"

"Why not," his grandfather had replied, answering the question with another question. "So, what's all the commotion about? You and your wife are grownups; you have two nice kids who are somewhat well adjusted and not too spoiled. You got a good job and, although I hate to admit it, you're almost as good a father to them as I was to you."

The voice, however, did not belong to his grandfather who, to Riley's knowledge, still had all of his fingers.

"Grab a hold, Junge," said the accented voice again, the hand with four and a half fingers beckoning to him. "If you stay down there much longer your hands and knees will sprout roots, and you'll become part of these here Superstitions."

"Superstitions," repeated Riley, the trepidation nudging fear out of the picture. "I thought I was on a roller coaster in Disney World whipping through Thunder Mountain."

"Don't reckon I ever heard of no Thunder Mountain," said the man. "And what's this Dizzy World? Ain't never heard of that either, Junge."

Riley thought for a moment, looked at the altered hand and grabbed it with his right hand. He felt himself being lifted off the ground almost like his sister used to lift her dolls off the living room carpet when he and Elsa used to rough house. "Disney World's a huge amusement park, Sir," said Riley sliding his hand from the man's grip. "And Thunder Mountain is a roller coaster ride there." He could see the old man's eyes analyzing, questioning and looking almost like his grandfather; except his grandfather's face didn't resemble the cracked leather on a saddle he thought he saw in Tumbleweed. His grandfather didn't have shaggy hair, a grey beard and talk with an accent. "I thought Thunder Mountain was where I was heading into Tumbleweed. Something must've happened."

"Something?" the old man asked. He gave a shrug. "Now

tumbleweeds I know. "Why would you want to go with those useless things?"

Riley shrugged and muttered, "I dunno, Sir."

The old man grinned. "Sir?" he repeated. You can call me, Dutch, Junge. Sir makes me sound older than I am."

"Sorry," apologized Riley. "But my father told me to always call any adult man, Sir." He quickly added. "Dad said that's the respectful thing to do."

"Your vater sounds like a gut man."

Riley heard the accented word and gave the old man a puzzled look.

"Vater is Deutsch for father."

Riley gave the old man another puzzled look.

"Deutsch is German," came the gravel coated explanation. "I'm German or Deutsch. I'm from Germany; Deutschland. That's why I'm called Dutch. Verstehen?"

Riley nodded even though he wasn't quite sure what the old man had said to him. "Kind of, Sir," said Riley. He gave the old man a puzzled look and asked, "Why do you keep calling me, Jungey?" he asked, his emphasis on the J and the e.

"Junge is another Deutsch word," said the old man. "You are a boy; a young man; a lad," came his heavy accented explanation. Verstehen?"

"Yes, Sir," replied Riley, then catching his error, quickly added, "Dutch."

"Das is gut," said the old man. "Yah."

Riley nodded and tried to smile. "Yah," he repeated beginning to feel more at ease around the old man. He pointed at himself and said, "My name is Riley." He stuck out his right hand and he and the old man shook hands.

"Riley," repeated the old man; "nice to know you." He rubbed at his beard. "Can't say that I ever heard that name before," he said. The old man's smile was concealed by his heavy grey beard. "Don't know where you're Thunder Mountain is, Lad," said Dutch, "but if you don't want to be eaten by a mountain lion or have Apache arrows piercing that skinny body of yours, you better follow me to the Dutchman. You'll be safe there for the night." He offered his right hand for Riley to shake. "My God given name is Jacob. "I'm Jacob Waltz."

"Dutchman?" asked Riley, his trepidation turning to a dissipating vapor. "The Lost Dutchman?" he asked, his question wedged between caution and excitement; his excitement winning out.

"Nothing lost about this Dutchman," said the man, giving a nod that Riley should follow him.

Riley didn't hesitate and followed the old man as the hot afternoon sun began its slow, cooling retreat to the west. He couldn't believe this was happening to him. One minute he was in a roller coaster car screaming and yelling; having a great time with his cousin and, in the next minute he was with an old man, Jacob Waltz, who called himself Dutch, heading for the Lost Dutchman mine. Was he dreaming?

"The mine is my home," said Dutch over his shoulder. "You should be safe there for tonight," he continued nonstop. "Don't know about tomorrow though. Tomorrows are always filled with surprises up here. If it's not with the Apaches scouting around these here parts, then it's those Cavalry horse soldiers snooping around. And, if not them, then there's a group of Mexicans mining for gold." He let out a laugh that sounded like a grunt. "All of them are looking for the same thing, Riley," he said, then pausing. "Gold."

Riley didn't hear Dutch's last word. He was too busy concentrating on another word. "Apaches?" asked Riley without breaking stride.

"Yep," said Dutch, respect coating his single word. "They can be ruthless if you get them upset. They're good people but you don't ever wanna get an Apache mad at you, Lad. Not if you know what's good for you."

"Oh, no, I won't, Sir."

Dutch let out a laugh. "They're not that bad," he said, pausing, thinking for a second and then continuing. "Just mad as a kicked hornet's nest because of what some of the palefaces did to them," he said. The old man shook his head slightly and continued talking, his heavy accent sometimes confusing Riley. "Those folks who call themselves politicians, you know, leaders of this country, seem to look the other way when the big business tycoons grab land from the various Indian tribes. They say those savages are in the way of progress."

"Tycoons," asked Riley politely.

"Old guys like me. Unlike me they have lots of money. I'm just some old guy who keeps looking for lots of money. That's why I live and work in the Dutchman. The mine's my home and it could make me a very rich man."

Riley surprised himself by asking: "If you were rich, Dutch, would you take land away from the Indians?"

Dutch let out a laugh. "No need to, Lad," he said, his voice sincere. "I'm not greedy. Some of those rich guys back east and the politicians, well, they're not only greedy, but they crave power."

Riley absorbed what he had just heard then replied, "My

grandfather read me a story once about a group of old men who sound like who you're talking about. They were called the Robber Barrons.

"Never heard of 'em," said Dutch.

They kept walking up the mountain following a trail much like the one he remembered walking with his grandfather. As they walked, Dutch continued to tell Riley about life on the mountain. "There's also a big family of Mexicans who are looking for gold up here. They ain't no trouble though. They work part of the mountain about three four miles from here. I guess they do okay or they wouldn't keep on digging there. Looking for gold ain't easy work, Lad."

Riley felt at ease with the old man. He still felt nervous and confused about what had happened. One minute he was riding a roller coaster ride with his cousin and then he found himself on all fours on a trail in the Superstition Mountains with an old miner. He couldn't help himself though so he continued to follow Jacob Waltz and felt he had been on this same trail before. Then he saw it. "Geez," he said and stopped cold.

Dutch turned around and looked at him. "You okay, Lad?" he asked.

Riley looked at him and then off to his left his eyes focused on a small stack of rocks only several inches high. "Dutch," he said carefully. "I think I've been on this trail before."

Silence greeted his comment and then the old man let out a sound like a grunt.

Riley pointed to the stack of rocks. "I made that Dutch," he said. "It's a cairn. I made it when I was up here with my grandfather about six weeks ago."

"You made that?" asked Dutch. Another combination grunt

and moan came from him. "I knew it t'weren't no Indian," he said, another grunt and moan coming from him. "They don't need no sign the size of Mount Moab to tell them where they're going or where they're at. Those folks can find their way using specks of dust and some bird droppings." He patted Riley on his head. "Do an old man a favor and take those rocks and give them a toss behind us, one at a time and not in the same place. That horse soldier scout is good but I don't want to make his job too easy."

Riley followed Dutch's instructions. His cairn went in three different directions; the last stone going over the side of the mountain.

"Are you tryin' to tell whoever's in these here mountains that we're inviting them for some beans tonight?"

Riley gave the old man a confused look. "Did I do something wrong?"

"Not really," the old man said, as he turned around and started walking. "You could've started a rock slide or a small avalanche," he said. Then he muttered, "macht micht," in his native tongue.

Riley felt bad but didn't know what to say or do. He kept following the old man up the trail. They had only gone several yards when the old man stopped and turned.

"Lad," he said. "Up here any noise can be heard at the ends of the earth. Understand?"

Riley's head went up and down once and he said softly, "I'm sorry."

"You can't be sorry for what you don't know. Sit down. Rest a spell," he advised.

Riley did so and looked admiringly at the old man who got

down on his haunches. "There's plenty of people who come up here snooping around hoping to find some gold. Some are hoping to find me. That, I guess, will guarantee them finding gold and getting rich." He let out a chuckle. "There's been plenty comin' around. They've never seen me, and they didn't find enough to buy a cup of coffee when they got back to civilization. Not even a half cup." He chuckled again. "I don't worry about dem dare folks. Most of them will get lost up here and all they'll find will be the Almighty." He shook his head from side to side. "I do worry about those Mexicans though. They keep getting closer and closer until one of these days I'll be sippin' Mescal with them in my heart."

"Your heart?" asked Riley, genuinely puzzled by the old man's comment. He pointed at his chest. "This heart?"

The old man's grin was visible through his beard and his shoulders shook. "No, Lad," he managed to say without gasping for breath. The Heart is a name I gave to the core area of my mine. It's where all the tunnels come together in one place like the veins in your body coming into your heart. It's where I eat and sleep. It's my home."

"Wow, you call where you live your Heart. That's so cool," replied Riley.

"Cool?" repeated Dutch.

"I mean your Heart sounds like a real nice place."

"Nice it is," said Dutch. He stood up, stretched and nodded at Riley so that they should continue on. "And, I want to keep it nice or cool, as you say. I don't need any visitors from south of the border, and I most certainly don't want no renegade horse soldiers who deserted their duty dropping in on me."

"Soldiers?" asked Riley, as he continued to be polite.

Somehow, his not being on a roller coaster ride with his family in Disney World hadn't sunk in. He was in another world, yet it was the same world he had been in with his grandfather six weeks earlier. His cairn told him that. "Are those soldiers you mentioned bad guys or good guys?"

"Nothin' good about those three," he replied. I've spotted them searching this mountain area, but they don't know where they're going. They could be trouble. All they ever do is shoot some small game for an evening meal and get drunk at night sitting around their campfire. Don't think them Apaches are too fond of them horse soldiers either. All of them make my life interesting up her. I'm glad to have your company. Whadda you say your name was?"

"Ah, Riley, Sir."

"Riley Sir?" asked Dutch with a chuckle. "Ain't ever heard no name like Riley Sir before. Where you from, Lad?"

Riley thought for a moment and said, "I'm from Chicago, Dutch."

The old man stopped, turned and looked at his young companion. "Where's this Chicago place and what are you doing here, Riley Sir?"

"My name is Riley," he said. "There's no Sir." He noticed Dutch's grin from behind his grey beard. "Chicago's my home. It's a big city on Lake Michigan."

"Heard of that lake," replied Dutch, turning and continuing hiking along what was supposed to be a trail. "Chicago I hear tell is an Indian name. Means smelly onions."

"Really?"

"I'm only telling you what I've heard, Riley. It's Riley, right?"

This time Riley laughed. "It's Riley."

"Well, Riley, whadda you doin' up in these here mountains by yourself?" asked Dutch.

Riley thought for a moment and said: "My grandma and grandpa live here in the state of Arizona; over in the west valley in Peoria." He pointed in what he thought was the west, but didn't see anything. "They live in a community called Trilogy."

"Arizona?" asked Dutch, as two other questions followed. "Peoria? Trilogy? What kind of a word is trilogy?" asked Dutch. "Never heard of it," he grumbled. "Never even seen it and I can see most everything out in this here valley from up here," he continued.

"Well, Dutch," began Riley.

Dutch gave a nod turned and said, "Later. We got us a way to go and don't have time right now for this Trilogy and Peoria stuff. Sounds like more smelly onions to me!"

They hiked in silence. Riley was in awe of the old man's agility and how his old boots didn't disturb a thing on the invisible trail. The sun continued its westward movement making their shadows more distinct and oblong. Riley was feeling thirsty and wondering how he had gotten up in the mountain without water. He had always carried at least two plastic bottles of water with him along with a lightweight hiker's backpack. His grandfather had warned him, ordered him, to drink plenty of water. "Have a wet belly before you head out in the desert," he had told Riley. "Bring plenty with you and leave a spare bottle or two in the car for when you get back. We don't have humidity out here like you do back in Chicago. If you dehydrate out on the trail, chances are you ain't comin' back."

Riley thought his grandfather was exaggerating and trying

to scare him back then on his first visit to Arizona. He was wrong. Well, kind of. Riley didn't heed his grandfather's advice and found himself down on all fours just as Dutch had found him. Only that time, his world began spinning around and before he hit the ground on his hands and knees, his backside had swiped the spines of a Cholla. That was a lesson he never forgot.

"How much farther, Dutch?" asked Riley, beginning to feel his mouth taste like the paste his teachers gave him during art activities in school. He tried to spit, but couldn't.

"Just up ahead," said Dutch, without looking back. "A stone's throw from here."

After what seemed forever Riley wondered just how strong of an arm Dutch had and what the size of the stone he was intending to throw. Then he began to feel signs of nausea. There was no water in sight and suddenly he realized he was following an old man who had a missing part of a little finger toward a mine that no one had ever seen. At least those were the stories he had read and heard about. Then he realized he had walked right smack into Jacob Waltz's backside.

"Whoa there, Lad," said Dutch, putting his hand on Riley's shoulder. "From here on follow me real close," he said in a hushed voice. "Step where I step. Twist when I twist and turn when I turn," he continued. "Verstehen?"

"Yes, Dutch, Sir," replied Riley, his voice a whisper as he fought off his body's need for water and the urge to turn the rocky, dusty ground into a bed. "Will there be some water after I get through stepping?" he asked.

"Water's just ahead," said Dutch. "You'll make it."

He believed the old man and followed his orders to the

letter; stepping, twisting and turning. His shoes were being placed precisely in the same spot as the old man's boot prints. Then he felt a cool breeze and in a blink he was in the entrance, a narrow, vertical slit cut by nature in between and behind two giant rocks.

"You okay, Lad?" asked Dutch.

"I'm good," said Riley, the drop in temperature reinvigorating him.

"Atta boy," said Dutch. "I've got a cistern over here with water. I collect rain water in it. Doesn't rain very often up here; couple times a year. But, when it does, a man feels like he's gonna get washed down the side of this here mountain."

Riley followed Dutch further into the cave until they stopped at a large pool looking like it had been carved out of a massive boulder. The pool was half filled with water. "So, that must be that cistern thing," thought Riley. There were several canteens off to the side and a couple of what looked liked puffed out animal skins hanging from rusted hooks that had been hammered into the rock. The skins, Riley learned, were filled with water. Riley saw a canteen being held out to him. He took it and drank greedily.

"Whoa, Lad," said Dutch, putting his hand on the canteen. "Slow down. Save some for the fishes." He laughed. "When you finish, you can help me get a fire goin'. I make a good pot o' beans. You must be hungry."

"Yes, Sir," replied Riley, corking the canteen and handing it back to Dutch. "Thank you, Sir," he said. Then catching his slip added, "Thank you, Dutch."

Riley couldn't believe he was sitting in a cave; the Lost Dutchman Mine, next to Jacob Waltz, the legendary Dutchman and eating beans. "Am I dreaming?" he thought. "When will I wake up?" A small fire and the old man's stories mesmerized him just like his grandfather's. Those stories had always been a treat for Riley, but they didn't compare with the narrative of coming to this country from Germany, the trip across the ocean, landing in New York and then going by horse drawn wagon to Pennsylvania and years later ending up in a territory that would eventually become Arizona.

"Riley," the old man said, the wide blade of a Buck knife he used for an eating utensil being removed from his mouth. "Do you know why we built a fire on this very spot?"

Riley had no idea. The Dutchman's lone spoon that he had been given was filled with a mound of steaming beans. Those were quickly jammed in his mouth to satisfy the growl coming from his stomach. He shook his head from side to side and belched, neglecting his mother's warning about manners and not to talk with his mouth full.

"Smoke," said Dutch. "Smoke's a dead giveaway that'll have every Indian and fortune hunter up here in less 'n day."

Riley swallowed and nodded.

"This here mine is honeycombed with nature's ventilation system," he said, waving his hand with the missing part of the little finger over his head in a circle. "There's got to be a dozen or so holes in this here big rock of a mine. The breeze coming through here takes our smoke in all different directions, thins it into wisps and then kind of coughs it out 'o here. The Apaches can't even see it and they got eyes like eagles." The old man wiped his mouth with the back of his hand and continued. "If them dare Apaches can't see it, ain't no Cavalry riders and Mexicans gonna see it neither," said Dutch, letting out a belch.

"Gotta always be careful up here, Riley," he said, beans visible on his beard. "Can't trust no one; not Mother Nature and not even God," he said, wiping the back of his hand across his mouth. "Verstehen?" he asked, using his favorite question.

Riley nodded, knowing what the old man was asking. He was about to shovel another spoon of beans into his mouth when he saw Dutch's index finger go to his lips.

The old man slowly stood up. Not a sound was made as he motioned to Riley to stay put. Riley was afraid to swallow because he might break the eerie silence that had settled in the cave. Only the fire's crackle could barely be heard as Dutch disappeared into the mine's blackness.

Riley sat as if he had become part of the mine's rock interior. His only movement came when he swallowed his beans and then felt himself choking and wanting to cough. He covered his mouth with both hands, swallowed several more times, felt his eyes tear up and the sensation to cough disappeared. He removed his hands and a roar of a cough and sneeze erupted from him. He wanted to die. He was petrified.

Thankfully, Dutch returned a short time later and sat down at the fire that was now embers. "I left you because I thought I heard something. Did too. It was those soldier's horses clip-clomping alongside the mountain. Made quite a racket," he continued. "Almost as loud as that animal sound you made, Lad." Dutch glared at Riley and then smiled. "Not to worry. Their horses never shied a bit. Not an ear twitched." Dutch gave a yawn and said, "We'll sleep right here tonight just in case those soldiers aren't as dumb as I think they are." His head rotated from left to right and back again. "We got us a half dozen or so routes to get out of here if we hear of anyone coming. Like I told you, this here mine is kind a like a human heart. Veins going out in all directions," he continued. "I've explored every one of them and I know this here mountain like the back of mien hand. If those soldiers or anyone else come a snoopin' around we got nothin' to worry about, Lad. I've got all kinds of surprises for intruders." Dutch stopped and seemed to listen with an intensity that concerned his young companion. "If there is trouble, I'll act as a decoy and you stay in the tunnel I send you in. Go to the very end. You'll be safe and I'll take care of our intruders." Dutch looked at him his eyes asking if Riley understood.

Riley nodded and had a feeling that he didn't want intruders coming into the mine.

Dutch looked at Riley. "Meant to ask you Lad, but I never saw clothes and shoes like you're wearing before," he said. "What's that DBacks thing written across your chest mean?"

"Those are the Arizona Diamondbacks," replied Riley, tracing the name across his red and white t-shirt with his index finger.

"You like them nasty rattlers?" asked Dutch, his head shaking from side to side.

"Oh, no," said Riley nonchalantly. "I'm a Cubs fan. My grandfather gave me this shirt last month when I was here with my family visiting him."

"He give you those kurze Hosen too?"

Riley gave him a blank look.

Dutch pointed at his short pants. "If they were made out of leather, you'd have Lederhosen," he said.

Riley grinned. "I get it," he said. My cargo shorts; the pockets," he said, flipping at the tops of the pockets on his shorts. "Yeah, Dutch, I get it. Cool, man." He continued to grin at the old man. "My mother bought them for me."

"Mmmm," muttered Dutch. "And where are your suspenders?" he asked. Then stretching out his red pair, he asked. "Aren't you afraid your pants are going to fall down?" He let out a chuckle.

"Nah."

"That must be your way of saying, nein." He chuckled again. "Lad," he said, "it looks like you're getting sleepy. I got a spare blanket you can sleep on. I just hope you don't snore."

"Does he really think I can sleep here," Riley thought to himself. Then his eye lids felt too heavy to stay open

Chapter 6

Sleep had no trouble taking over Riley. He had wrapped himself up in the old torn blanket Dutch gave him and didn't mind the smell of what seemed like a herd of cows he once saw in a friend of his father's barn on a dairy farm in Bloomer, Wisconsin. Actually, the blanket's smell was worse and Riley thought it had been probably used on one of Dutch's mules that the old man told him about just before they both dozed off.

Riley hadn't given any thought about how the old man originally got to his mine and up into the Superstition Mountains. Dutch's transportation had been on horseback towing two loaded down mules behind his horse. The horse had died first. Normally sure-footed, Fritz the horse had broken both front legs the day before Dutch had found the mine entrance. He had no choice but to put the animal out of his misery. It was a reluctant rifle shot but he had saved much of the meat, carrying it up to the mine and his new found Heart. One trip was all he could make before both air and land scavengers turned Fritz into a skeleton of polished bones. As Riley learned before dozing off, Dutch had salted and cured the meat preserving what he could.

Riley was too tired to mind the hard, cool ground that was his mattress. He was asleep and dreaming of the roller coaster at Thunder Mountain in Disney World, speeding along in the last car; he and William screaming for all they were worth. He felt his body twisting, turning and being jarred as the ride sped through the town of Tumbleweed. "William, cut it out," he said to his cousin. "Stop poking me." He felt himself being tossed and turned. "I told you to stop pokin'...." He felt a hand over his mouth and his eyes popped open. It was Dutch's hand.

Dutch had the index finger of his other hand to his lips, a look of concern on his face. His head went slowly from side to side before he removed his hand from Riley's mouth. The index finger at his lips turned into a curl beckoning Riley to get up and follow him.

Riley didn't make a sound as he followed Dutch into the tunnel that Dutch had indicated earlier that they would use in case of trouble. He followed in Dutch's footsteps, aping his every move, remembering the instructions he had received before they started the final leg of the trek to the concealed mine.

Dutch stopped and so did Riley. He bent forward and whispered to Riley. "We got visitors, Lad."

Riley's eyes asked his question.

"I guess those soldiers heard your choke and cough. Didn't think they did. Sly ones they are," continued Dutch, his whisper barely audible. "Musta been that Indian scout. He can hear a coyote yelp all the way to Mexico."

Riley's eyes grew big but he didn't speak.

"He was leading them other two," Dutch continued to whisper. "Should a known. He was wearin' this cap called a Kepi. Them two others was wearin' standard Cavalry hats. That scout had this long black hair tied behind his head. Yeah, he's a sly one alright."

Riley still didn't speak. He listened intently to what Dutch was saying to him; the old man's whisper even lower, his mouth almost against Riley's ear. The instructions were simple. He was to take the tunnel to the end and stay there. "Sit tight," Dutch told him. "And, regardless of what you hear don't move from the end of that dare tunnel. Verstenhen?"

Riley's head barely moved up and down. "Get a move on," he heard Dutch tell him, and he got a move on.

The tunnel was so black Riley thought he knew how a blind person felt. He stepped gingerly as he placed his right hand against the rough rock wall, his finger tips guiding the way, tracing his course to the end. He could feel a slight draft coming through the tunnel, the side of the tunnel coarse, even jagged in spots. Each step of his hiking boots came down carefully anticipating unseen objects in his path. There were none. Not any he could step on. He barely breathed as he continued on for what seemed like an eternity. Then he almost jumped out of his skin. What sounded like a roar of thunder echoed through the hollowed out vein of rock he was in. "A gun shot?" he asked silently. "Sounded like one," his answer coming back in silence. Then he jumped even higher this time as another roar of thunder rumbled through the mine. He stopped and froze unsure of what to do. Then he remembered Dutch's instructions and he continued forward, each step careful as before, his hand guiding his way along the rough side of the tunnel. He thought he saw a trace of what had to be moonlight coming through a crack in the tunnel. The sliver of light was above and ahead of him. "Probably another entrance like the other one," he thought, as he continued on toward an end that wasn't coming as fast as he had hoped. He kept his eyes glued on the ray of light and suddenly it was gone. Before he realized what had happened something grabbed his neck from the side. The something was a human hand and it stopped him with such force that his hiking boots left the ground without making a sound. The hand did not belong to Dutch.

"Not so fast, Little Bear Cub," said a voice, that reminded Riley of hearing Indians talk in some of the old western movies he and his cousins had watched on television when they would go to each others' houses to hang out. The hand squeezed his neck even harder. "Come!"

Riley was stunned. He was too scared to question the heavy accented single order. Not with a hand about to turn his neck into the size of his thumb. The first thing he could think of was to ask a silent question: "How did this guy know I cheer for the Bears and the Cubs?" Then Dutch's instructions hit him, but those instructions didn't say anything about waiting with a stranger who was making it difficult for him to breathe. The stranger was indeed an Indian, the one Dutch had described as wearing the hat called a Kepi. A ray of light from the breech in the cave temporarily illuminated the top half of Riley's captor. The voice sounded like what Riley thought an Indian's voice should. The Indian's hand squeezed Riley's neck harder, his ability to breathe being taken away. Riley managed to turn his shoulders, his head barely moving with them. It was enough for him to see the ray of moonlight illuminating his strangler from the shoulders up. "Oh, God," thought Riley. "It's the Indian Dutch said had the black braid down his back; the one who really is an Indian scout for the Cavalry."

"Lead the way, Little Bear Cub," said the Indian, giving Riley a shove in the direction he just came. "Take me to the old man's gold."

Riley tried to struggle, but the Indian held him even tighter. "Oh, crap," he said silently again, thinking while trying not to panic. Then it hit him and he almost started laughing. His grandfather had once told him along with Elsa and his mother how to protect themselves if they were ever accosted by a man.

"All men have an Achilles Heel," his grandfather had started out. "Even you, Elsa," he said, "can be stronger than the strongest man." The three of them had looked at him and listened. "You don't have to have a gun, or a knife, or a hand grenade or the biggest club in the world. Little David slew Goliath with a rock and his sling shot." He paused and looked at the three of them. You don't need that. No siree, you don't." There was another pause. "All you need are three things." There was another pause. "And I'm going to tell you what those three things are."

Riley's grandfather started out by saying, "First, you need what's called the element of surprise. How you do that is up to you." There was another of his hesitations and he said, "Second, you take whatever hard object you have; that includes your fist, a stone if you have David's sling shot; your purse, ladies, if you carry one with some weight in it. Whatever." There had been a twinkle in his eyes when he stated emphatically, "Third, you take that hard object of yours and you hit that man as hard as you can between his legs with an upward punch. I mean punch him hard." Riley recalled the speed at which his grandfather's fist sailed upward from the ground to waist high as he demonstrated his hard punch. His grandfather had smiled then. "Oh, yes, one more thing, a fourth element; you run like the dickens as soon as you hear a moan come from that bad guy's mouth. And there will be a moan. There will also be a whoosh of air."

"Surprise," thought Riley. "How am I gonna surprise an Indian?"

Riley didn't have to. Two pushes from the Indian later, Riley stumbled on an errant rock that was in the middle of the tunnel. He dropped to his knees, but the Indian was way too strong, his grip never loosening on Riley's neck. The Indian treated Riley like his sister treated her doll, yanking her up. He was being yanked up much harder; by his neck. In order to lift Riley and get him on his feet the Indian bent his knees and went into a slight squat. At that moment Riley made a fist with his right hand and shot an uppercut toward where he thought the Indian's legs divided. What followed surprised both Riley and the Indian. As his grandfather had predicted, there was a rush of air from the Indian that was joined by an immediate excruciating moan. Riley was no longer being strangled, and the Indian was down on his knees. In an instant, Riley took off like a scared rabbit yelling at the top of his voice, "Dutch! Save me, Dutch!" His right hand bounced off the side of the tunnel wall as he ran through the dark tunnel. He heard another groan and then the sound of running feet. The Indian was no longer surprised. Angry was more like it.

"Dutch!" Riley continued to scream, feeling out of breath and hearing the footsteps behind him gaining ground. The sound of the Indian's breathing was getting closer, his sounds nowhere near as labored as Riley's. "Dutch!" he yelled again, as he brushed against an object that was not rock or stone. He took several more strides and then heard the deafening sound of thunder again. This time he knew it wasn't thunder, but the sound of a gun, he thought; a big gun.

Riley stopped and listened. The only thing he heard was his heavy breathing. He put his hands on his knees to catch his breath and listened harder. He thought he heard the faint scrapping of something being drug along the ground. "Oh, God, now what?" he thought. He stood like he was made out of stone, motionless, barely breathing. He listened harder. The scrapping sound had disappeared. Then he almost let out a scream. A hand had settled on his shoulder.

"Lad," the familiar voice said. "Are you alright?"

Chapter 7

"Is that really you, Dutch?" asked Riley, fighting back his tears. "Oh, God, is it really you?"

"It's me, Lad, and I'm not God," said Dutch, playfully mussing up Riley's hair. "No need to worry now. Ain't no bad guys going to cause you no harm."

Riley could barely make out the old man's features in the dark. He was thankful for the lack of light that now hid his tears. "Thank you, Dutch," he sniffled, his fists gouging at his eyes.

"No need for dunka," said Dutch. "Those horse soldiers aren't going to hurt anybody."

Riley's tears stopped in an instant. "You mean those soldiers are…." He couldn't finish his question.

"They are," said Dutch, providing the answer to Riley's truncated question. "The Indians like to say they're in the Happy Hunting Ground." Dutch let out a slight cough. "Well, Kepi Black Braid, the Indian is. I don't know about those other two. I have a feeling that they were not thinking about anything happy when they were getting ready to send us into das Jenseits."

"They were going to kill us?" asked Riley, horrified that someone wanted to take away his life. "Really?"

Dutch let out a chuckle. "I bet you never thought a cough and a choke would be the cause of the end of you."

Riley's feeling of being scared was shoved out of the picture by awe. He was still excited and his hands trembled. "Did you really," said Riley slowly, being cautious. "Did you really shoot them?" He could see the worn soles of two pairs of boots; the toes sticking straight up as if at attention.

"Nein," said Dutch, his head barely going from side to side. "I ain't never shot another human being in my life," he said. "I heard those two horse soldiers making their way toward me I thought I might have to. They weren't very quiet about what they were planning to do once they found me. Evil they were." He paused. "That's when I heard that noise that sounded like an explosion, seemed to come from the bowels of this mountain. Hurt my ears and made my head pound. Then there was a second explosion. That one knocked me to my knees. My head was ringing like some Friar was calling an entire Mexican village to come to church by ringing the bells and my head was stuck up in the bell tower. You sure you're okay?" he asked Riley.

Riley nodded and asked, "If you didn't shoot them, then who did?"

"Good question, Lad," the old man said. His hand traveled head high along the wall where they were standing. He found a candle and lit it. "I'm not sure it was someone shooting a gun," he said. "Kind of sounded like it, but it was different. I know the sound my rifle makes. Had to shoot a cougar once that got in here one night and wanted to have me for supper. That was only one shot. Those two explosions were louder; more like the sound of dynamite going off when I have to blast in the tunnel I'm digging in."

Riley jumped. "Are those the two soldiers?" he asked,

pointing; his hand shaking and his eyes bigger than the metal plate he had eaten beans from earlier. "Are they...?"

"Looks like it," said Dutch, squatting alongside the first body; the second body several steps behind the first laying with his head in the same direction. He gazed upon the first soldier, the candle light flickering on a face that showed intense fear. The candle lit up the second man's face. There was a second look of fear like a grotesque mask on that man's face. Dutch went back to the first dead man, rolled him over and ran the candle from the back of his head to the heels of his boots. He did the same with the second man. Then Dutch sat down on the ground and placed the candle alongside the nearest dead soldier. "Lad, I don't see any trances of blood. Not a drop. These men couldn't have been shot. Whatever killed them wasn't my doin'. What I do know is I didn't shoot them. The only other time I've ever fired my rifle outside of that cougar I told you about was to shoot a Javelina for food. Smelly critter. Ugly too. Meat wasn't bad once it was burned over a fire. No siree, Lad I didn't shoot either of those two soldier boys. Not that I wouldn't have if it meant saving our hides from those three. Evil is what they were. Downright evil."

Riley thought for a moment and then cautiously asked, "If they weren't shot, they how did they die?"

Dutch got to his knees and sat back on his heels. He laughed. "Don't ever sit like this, Lad, if you're wearin' spurs."

Riley didn't see the humor and repeated his question: "How did those three guys die, Dutch? Do you know?"

Dutch sat silent, pondering Riley's question. "Well," he started out then adding a pause. "Now don't you go getting' scared on me."

"Scared," Riley blurted out. "I was about to be scalped. How much scareder can a person get?"

"Do you believe in ghosts?" asked Dutch, his voice calm and gentle.

"Ghosts?" repeated Riley not knowing what to think. "I dunno."

Dutch sat silent for a moment, the candle's flame flickering off his shaggy beard. "When I first came to this mountain and started looking for gold I heard a rumor that ghosts or spirits or somethin' that wasn't human or real had put a curse or somethin' on this mountain. I thought the story was a lot of hearsay and nonsense; folks tryin' to keep outsiders like me from discovering the huge mother lode that was buried here."

"Mother lode?" repeated Riley.

"That's another name for the biggest, the largest and the best vein of gold anyone has ever seen. It's a miner's dream come true. Find the mother lode and you'll be rich beyond your wildest dreams."

"Is there a mother lode here?"

"Could be," said Dutch. "Don't know for sure. I've found some gold, but no mother lode. That's why I'm still up her lookin' and diggin'." He stroked at his beard for a moment. "What I do know, Riley is that those ghosts or spirits or whatever must've takin' a likin' to me because I've never been harmed by anything or anyone since I've been here and I've been here about as many years as you are old."

"Ghosts protected you?" asked Riley, his curiosity getting the better of him. "From what?"

Dutch thought about Riley's question. "Well, there was a cave in once in one of the tunnels. Just before it happened I heard what sounded like a loud voice. It hollered out what sounded like, 'Run!' It wasn't like the ones we heard that ended the lives of these three. I dropped my pick and ran toward the mine opening. Just as I hit daylight, the ceiling of the mine came crashing down; a ton of rock landing where I had been working."

"Really?"

Dutch nodded. "Then there was a time a couple of Banditos found the mine entrance. They were carrying enough guns and ammunition on them to start a revolution. Well, I went off to hide. And, you know what, just as those two got into the mine a ways there were two claps of thunder; loud ones like the ones you and I heard. When the Banditos didn't show up I went to check out their whereabouts. I found them just like we found those three."

"But why are you being protected? Why was I saved?"

"I guess the spirits know we don't mean no harm. They probably understand we're church going people even though I haven't been to church in years. I did go all the time when I was a young boy in Germany; went with my parents, my mother especially. She always told me that I should do unto others like the Good Book said. Love and respect all of God's creatures; all of what he created. I've always done that. You don't know how much it hurt me to put my horse out of her misery. I cried after. I even prayed that God would make a better place for her to live." He paused and gave Riley a serious look, more serious than he had every received from his grandfather or his father. "Never told this to a livin' soul," he continued. "But, I knelt and prayed; cried my eyes out for that horse." He stopped and looked around. "I swear I thought I heard others crying with me."

"Really?"

"Really," said Dutch. "So when I tell you I didn't shoot no one I hope you believe me."

"I believe you."

They sat in silence until Riley's back side seemed to be filled with pins and needles. He stood up and stretched. "Oh, geez," he muttered.

"Somethin' wrong, Lad?" asked Dutch as he stood up.

Riley nodded in the direction of where the soles of a pair of moccasins were looking back at him. "Are we just gonna let him stay there?"

"Nah," replied Dutch. "As evil as those men were, they deserve a Christian burial." He indicated with his thumb pointing over his right shoulder at the other two bodies lying behind him. "I'll need your help to get them outta here so I can pray over them. Don't want those three stinkin' up the place. This is my home. You've heard the old saying that home is where the heart is," he said. He stopped and waited for a reply that was in the form of his young companion's head going slowly up and down. "Gut."

Riley listened to Dutch explain what he was to do to help. He never thought that going on the Thunder Mountain roller coaster would include dragging a dead body—by the heels no less—along a dark tunnel to what Dutch had called, Das Chute.

Das Chute, it turned out, was a circular opening in the mountain wall just big enough for objects no bigger than a mule or, in this case, the bodies of three evil killers to be shoved through. Once through, they would drop down a rock channel that nature had cut over a million years. It was like a giant version of slides in the playground across from his house. The chute, as he found out, ended on the floor of the canyon. "Saves me lots of haulin'," explained Dutch. "I do go down and clean up real good. Don't want no pryin' eyes getting' to curious as to where waste came from. What I might miss, the animals and birds will clean up. "Don't worry, Lad, we'll bury those three real proper like. Every man, good or evil, should have the words from the Good Book read over them before they get returned to the earth. You ever heard of the words, ashes to ashes and dust to dust, Lad?"

"Sort of," said Riley.

"Good. Now grab dat dare pair of moccasins by da heels and start draggin'."

Riley had struggled, the sheer weight of the scout making him strain and labor like he had never done before in his life. He was sweating and panting and puffing even harder than when he was running for his life from the human being he was now dragging down the tunnel the old miner had indicated.

Riley was surprised at Dutch's strength. The old man was dragging both soldiers at the same time. Riley couldn't figure out how he could do it until they got to the circular opening and the light made it possible for Riley to see that Dutch was wearing a harness.

"Belonged to my last mule," he explained. "I've used it plenty since she left me."

Riley could see that the opening in the rock was at a severe angle making it almost impossible to see anything below or off to the horizon. He had no idea as to what direction he was looking.

"Okay, Lad," said Dutch, very serious. "I'll take it from here. You go on back to the Heart and see if you can get a fire going for cookin'. We've had a long night with way too much excitement for an old geezer like me and I'm hungry."

"You sure you don't need any help?" asked Riley, feeling relieved, even though very curious as to what the old man would do next.

"I'm sure," he said, as he removed the harness from around his shoulders and stretched. "Off with you now. I've got some praying to do for these souls. Lord knows they need it."

As Riley made the first curve in the tunnel, he heard what he knew was the sound of heels being scraped in the dirt. He slowed down his pace, his right hand in contact with the rough tunnel wall and listened. There was Dutch's unmistakable grunt, more sliding and a second grunt. Riley listened. Nothing. Then he heard what he knew was the first of the evil men hitting the ground below. At first he thought it was all three men bouncing off rocks to the bottom until he realized it was one body bouncing several times. He heard another grunt and knew what would follow. He also knew that he had better follow Dutch's orders. His stomach also told him to get going.

He was back in the heart of the mine in no time. Scraps of timbers were gathered for a fire and he thought he could start it the way Dutch had. But he didn't have on a coarse pair of pants to strike a match; only his hiking shorts. Besides, he didn't have any of the stick matches that Dutch used. Then he felt it. His arrowhead. He pulled it from his pocket, got on his hands and knees and began feeling for a rock in the dark. There were several he grabbed. "Ah, come on, be there," he blurted out, crawling on his bare knees on the rocky floor. "I know you're there." One hand swept in front of the other as he crawled along. "Gotcha," he said, as his fingers dug into a small pile of straw that Dutch told him about, the straw once used to feed his mule. Riley went to where the fire wood was stacked in a waiting pyramid. He took out his arrowhead, picked up a rock, made a wish attached to a prayer and struck the rock against the arrowhead. Nothing happened. He tried the striking again. Nothing happened. "Stupid rock," he muttered, as he tossed the stone aside. He grabbed a second stone. Three unsuccessful tries later that rock joined the first one. "Come on, Riley," he muttered. "Two strikes on you. Come on, you know you can hit this guy. He ain't got any stuff on his pitches." His arrowhead and stone came in contact and there was a spark. "Wow," he yelled out. "It really works. Grandpa was right."

The straw was soon smoldering and the fire burning when Dutch returned. "Good Lad," he said to Riley. "Knowing how to start a fire with a flint will help keep you alive in these here mountains." Dutch went to a corner of the cave, removed some rocks and reached into a hole in the ground. He pulled out a heavy cast iron pot and placed it next to the fire. "Hope you don't mind beans again," he said as he removed the heavy lid. "Won't make no difference if you do or you don't. That's all we got until I can shoot us some meat."

"Shoot?"

Chapter 8

Riley didn't need to be told to get some sleep. His eye lids felt as if they weighed as much as he did. He was exhausted.

Sleep came easy at first. Then he began to toss and turn. His body wasn't used to small stones and pebbles digging into his sides and back. One thing kept going through his mind and that one thing was a series of exploding sounds. Even though he had never heard the real sound of a gunshot, he was positive the thundering noises that caused the tunnel to vibrate when he was being chased came from a gun; a big gun; one just like he had seen leaning against the wall of the Heart. He tossed and turned even more. At one point, he almost ended up in the smoldering ashes of the fire that the Dutchman had used to heat up his blackened cast iron pot containing the thick, chewy beans for their dinner.

As the sounds continued to rattle in his dream, he could see the three evil soldiers lying in the two tunnels. But in his dream the soldiers weren't dead. They were all smiling at him; the Apache scout's perfect white teeth grinning at him, being joined by a smile outlined with brown teeth and another mouth with a hideous, crooked smile; half the teeth gone.

He awoke with a start to see Dutch sitting Indian style by the fire that was burning brightly. The pot of beans from the night before was on the fire, the beans simmering and steaming.

Quickly he was wide awake. He watched Dutch run a rag along a metal object that looked like the old man's rifle. That sight quickly cleared the Sandman's handiwork from his eyes and made him feel more than awake. He thought for a moment, pretended to yawn and said, "Is it morning already?" Then he faked another yawn.

"Yah," said Dutch, without looking up. "Guten Morgen, sleepyhead," said his low accented voice. "Hungry?"

"Kind of," said Riley, as he watched the rag polish the gun's barrel first and then move to the wooden stock of the repeating rifle. "You going out hunting for meat?" asked Riley. "I thought that's what you told me last night about using your rifle."

"Nein," said Dutch, standing up and placing the rifle against the nearest wall of the cave. "Can't shoot a gun up here without looking in all directions first," he said. "The sound of this here repeating rifle going off in these mountains would bring the entire U.S. Cavalry plus the Apache tribe and every Mexican north of the border searching for gold. You remember those noises from last night, don't you?"

"I had dreams about them all night," said Riley, then stretching and letting out a yawn. "I thought you told me those weren't gun shots," he said, as he sat back on the heels of his hiking boots, his blanket acting as a kneeler for his bare knees. "Those explosions didn't come from the ghosts you told me about who protected you, did they?"

"That they did," said Dutch.

"Really?" asked Riley, now fully awake.

Dutch gave a nod and removed a large buck knife from a sheath belted to his pants, stuck it in the kettle and gave the beans a couple of stirs. "And last night they protected us, did they not?"

"I guess," said Riley starting to feel uneasy.

"I guess too," said Dutch. He took the broad blade of the knife and began to use it to transfer beans to their metal plates. "Plop" went the sound of the beans as they hit the plate. Several plops later Dutch handed one of the plates to Riley. "Eat hardy, Lad," said Dutch. "We got three graves to dig after breakfast. The turkey vultures and some of the other scavengers will be settling in for a big feast if we don't hurry up and get those three corpses in the ground. Circling birds bring more than four legged visitors. Besides the Indians and those three dead horse soldiers, we don't want the Pedraza family barging in on us. Those folks have been looking around here for gold for years. Them and another Mexican clan named Peralta." Dutch paused and filled his plate. "I heard they found some gold. Not the mother lode, but enough to have every family member from south of the border up here wanting to get rich. Some of them have come snooping around like them three soldiers did. They keep getting closer and closer. They're like Blood Hounds. I sure hope our friendly spirits will protect us from the likes of them. Some of them men carry rifles like mine and wear at least two bandoleers each."

"Bandoleers?" asked Riley cautiously.

"Leather belts holding lots of bullets," said Dutch as he wiped his buck knife clean on his trousers. "Enough chit-chat, Lad," he ordered. "Essen."

Riley understood that he was being told to eat from Dutch's gestures. He stuffed his mouth with an overflowing spoon of beans; the beans still steaming hot. Riley didn't care. He was starving.

"As soon as you finish," said Dutch, "grab one of those picks and a long handle shovel stacked on that wall and come with me."

Riley struggled with the heavy pick and the awkward long handle shovel as he tried to keep up with Dutch. The path inside was easy, seeming to run down hill over a series of switch backs—a back and forth route to make footing easier and prevent taking a high speed tumble down the interior of the mountain. Riley kept banging the shovel off the wall by accident that, at one point, had Dutch stopping and turning. "Hey, Lad, our friends the ghosts need their rest too. Keep banging that shovel off the rocks and you might end up like those three dead soldier friends of ours."

"Sorry," muttered Riley. For the first time since he met Dutch on the trail after somehow being detoured from the Thunder Mountain roller coaster, he missed his family. The beginning of 'Why' and 'What' questions started to formulate in his mind. He couldn't believe this was real. His questions stopped with a wry smile when he thought, "Oh, man, is William ever gonna be jealous of me."

The remainder of the trip to the outside of the mine and the end of Das Chute went on in silence. Riley struggled to keep the two tools he carried from disturbing any ghosts. Once at the entrance, the sun blinding them both for a moment, Dutch stood in the shadows of the opening. In no more than a minute, he raised his right hand and gave it a gentle move forward. "All clear, der Bub," he announced.

Riley followed him through a tight separation between two giant boulders. Dutch squeezed his way through sideways, inhaling, sometimes squatting and wiggling his way through. Riley got through with the rocks barely touching him. More large rocks had formed a natural tunnel, the height ten to twelve feet tall; the sides about the width of Dutch's shoulders. The tunnel had a gentle curve to the right. They had walked about a hundred yards when Dutch came to a stop, his right hand going up; an indicator to Riley to stop where he was at. There appeared to be a sharp turn to the right and Dutch disappeared from sight after taking a couple of steps. Then a hand appeared and motioned for Riley to continue.

Riley noticed the faint aroma the moment he made the sharp turn and stood alongside of Dutch. "Is that what I think it is?" he asked.

Dutch nodded and walked slowly ahead until the path turned sharply to the left. When Riley got to the turn the natural rock roof over the tunnel disappeared and he could look up and see the sky. He could also see a long curving groove in the rocks that climbed up the side of the mountain. Or, its course ran down the side of the mountain from high up; a slit in the rocks above appeared to be an opening. Riley realized that's where Dutch's Das Chute began and that it ended where the three dead men had been sent on their first leg to the Happy Hunting Ground.

The digging was grueling work. Riley found himself working harder than he ever had in his life. He was sweating; his Diamondbacks t-shirt showing the perspiration stains around the neck. The shovel was useless against the ground. The pick was doing the job of digging into the rock as they dug a pit big enough for the three dead renegade killers. Riley stopped shoveling when the blade of his shovel came up with several bones. "Dutch," he blurted out; the shovel sticking out horizontal, one of the bones having fallen to the ground.

"Fritzie," muttered Dutch. "Dig more in my direction," he said calmly. "I don't want those three contaminating my horse. She's too good to be in the same ground as those three devils."

Riley felt exhilarated swinging the heavy pick when they had started. He made a game out of driving the heavy sharp point into the ground; pretending he was a strong man at an amusement park swinging a giant mallet trying to send a tiny ball skyrocketing upward to ring a brass bell. Now, as his sweat had turned his Diamondback's t-shirt into a dripping rag, he was in need of a drink of water. The novelty of his brass bell game had turned stale and he was wondering when Dutch would say they were finished digging the grave. No sooner had he thought about the digging being over and it was.

"That should about do her," said Dutch, leaning against his long handle shovel. "Don't need to go no deeper. "We'll stack plenty of rocks over them three. No animals will get at them; neither will unwelcome eyes. And the only ones who can come a spying on us would have to be someone your age and weight. No adults could crawl through that opening to get here."

Riley felt relieved when Dutch told him that he wouldn't have to be a part of the actual burial. The three bodies scared him and turned his stomach. If Dutch didn't want his help moving them and placing their remains in the grave, that was alright with him. Then he was surprised at what Dutch said next.

"Der Bub," he said, without looking at Riley. "Go back and squeeze your way back through that rock. Just as you get into the tunnel you'll see my rifle. Bring it to me."

"Rifle?" repeated Riley. He never saw a rifle being carried by Dutch or didn't think he saw it when they were coming down to dig the grave. "Sure, Dutch. I'll be right back."

He traced the route back, getting through the narrow slit in the rock with no problem. The rifle was exactly where Dutch said it would be, standing at attention, waiting to be called into action. Riley was careful not to touch the metal barrel, but kept his hands on the wooden stock. He had to slide the rifle along the ground ahead of him to get it through the opening in the rock, but quickly wiped it off with his t-shirt. When he got back to the area where they had been digging he found Dutch reading from his Bible, a pile of rocks covering the grave, the mound barely visible. Then he heard Dutch say, "Rest in peace. Amen."

"That's it?" asked the boy, wondering what was next. He didn't wait long.

"I want you to take the tools, mine and yours, back to the Heart and stack 'em up. You know how they go. Get yourself some water too. You earned it this morning. And, der Bub, don't worry about waking up the ghosts with all your clanging and banging. They're up. They'll watch out over you. Just don't go jumpin' out of your skin if you hear any explosions."

"Where are you going, Dutch?" asked Riley. "I don't like being in the Heart all alone."

"I'm going out scouting and do some hunting for our dinner tonight. "Me think you're getting kind of tired of beans. I know I am." He patted Riley on the head. "I'll be back about sundown," he explained. "If you get bored, go do some exploring. But, be careful. Take a couple of candles. You know where they're at. Go down that one tunnel where you met your Apache friend last night," he said, with an impish grin. "You know; the one where he chased you. Maybe he has a vetter."

"A what?" asked Riley noticing Dutch's grin getting bigger.

"A cousin; a family member," said Dutch, almost laughing. "Maybe a twin."

"Very funny," said Riley.

"Yah, funny," repeated Dutch. "Just be careful and don't lose your sense of direction from the Heart. A man can get lost real easy if he don't pay no attention to where he's at."

"I'll be careful," said Riley, not liking the idea of being alone all day in the mine but, at the same time, his adventurous side wanting to explore every inch of the maze of tunnels. He told himself that there would be all sorts of exciting things in the veins that led from the Heart leading him to places not even his grandfather had seen in his lifetime or even knew about. "I'll be careful, Dutch," he said. "And I won't get the ghosts mad at me. I promise."

"Gut," said Dutch putting a canteen with a strap over his shoulder and picking up his rifle. "Come, walk with me."

Riley had followed the old man along a tunnel that turned out to be the same one they had used when he first followed him into the mine's hidden opening. Before he left he stuffed two candles and some matches into the pockets of his hiking shorts. He remembered the opening in the rocks and accompanied Dutch to the trail.

"Be careful, der Bub," said Dutch. "And you might want to get down on your knees and use your hands to brush away our boot prints as you back into that opening to head into the mine."

"I will," said Riley, already getting to his knees; his hand sweeping at the rocky ground.

"And, der Bub," the Dutchman continued, a twinkle in his eyes, "don't be shy about picking up a rock or two to add to your arrowhead. Consider it a gift from me."

Riley nodded as he continued sweeping away any evidence from the rocky ground that anyone had been there. "Thank you, Dutch, Sir."

"Auf Wiedersehen."

Riley cast a nervous smile, looked down and made a few more sweeps to the ground with his hands and, when he looked back up, Dutch was gone. Also gone was the feeling of fear, that replaced by one of superiority that crept over him. Even though the mine wasn't his, he suddenly felt it was. He was the master; the ruler; the king. No one could see him, but he could see everything and everyone for miles around once he got back inside and could look out of the openings he knew about.

He didn't need the candles to get back to the Heart. The

bright light that managed to penetrate the opening in the tunnel provided a gloomy route for him to follow most of the way. He used one hand like he had before to guide himself once the gloom turned to black and, before he realized, he was back in the main part of the mine. "Hello, Heart, old friend," he said with a touch of bravado. "I'm back."

Riley spent a few minutes thinking about where he would explore. Should he go and retrace where he had already been or should he take on new adventures? He had been in three of the six tunnels that led from the Heart. There was the one he had just used; the one that led to the path where he had found himself the day before when he met Dutch. One of the tunnels had led to Das Chute and the other, well, that's where he found himself in the grasp of an Indian scout for the U.S. Cavalry. Riley looked around, his gaze stopping at the entrance to each of the three unexplored tunnels, his mind asking in his youthful way, "Eeeny, meeny, myny, moe?" It didn't take him long to make his choice. "I'll go down each one," he muttered to the empty Heart.

When he got into the first tunnel, Riley lit a candle and walked along a narrow, winding course filled with loose gravel and small rocks designed to sprain or break an ankle if the explorer wasn't careful. The candle showed that there were places along the wall that looked like they had been attacked by a pick, digging for what had to be gold. Before he knew it, the tunnel ended at a jagged wall, piles of rock at the base, a half of what looked like a shovel handle lying in the rubble. His eyes searched the tunnel's end from top to bottom and he quickly lost interest. As he turned to head back the candle light bounced off something that caught his eyes. Curious, he bent down and picked up a small rock not quite the size of the major league autographed baseball his grandfather had given him as a memento of his visit to Arizona. The ball had been signed by many of the Chicago Cub players participating in spring training in Mesa. He held the rock in the light for a moment and then put it in his pocket, the same pocket with his arrowhead. Turning, he made his way back to the Heart.

"Now what," he said to the Heart, a slight echo taking place. He grinned and yelled out, "Hello!" The word bounced off the walls of the Heart reverberating into a series of slowly dwindling, "Hello's"and he said, "Cool." Then he cupped his hands to his mouth and let out a scream, this one louder than when he called for Dutch when he was being chased by the Indian. A series of, Hello-hello-hello roared back, the last hello losing most of its zip. "Cool, man," he said, and then he thought he heard something. His ears strained for a sound. There was none. "But I heard something," his brain said to him. "I know I heard something." He looked at the two remaining unexplored tunnels and started for the one to his right. "Nah," he said, stopping dead in his path. "It came from there," he corrected, looking toward the left hand tunnel. He didn't hesitate, his left hand going to his pocket to check and see if the candles and matches were still there. He could feel his arrowhead and his special rock in the other.

Riley followed a course that took him down hill and from right to left and then left to right. He did the back and forth, right left and left right movements for what seemed like several dozen times. Then he heard a sound. "It couldn't be," he said quietly. "No echo goes on that long." He inched ahead. Then he heard it again. He knew he wasn't hearing things. The word coming through the tunnel was, "Hello." He froze in place. He heard the word again. It was faint; far away, but it was, "Hello." Riley didn't move a muscle. He was too afraid. The first thought that came to him was that he was trespassing on sacred ground and that the ghosts were giving him a friendly warning. He thought for a moment and muttered, "It can't be. Ghosts wouldn't say hello if they were warning me to keep out. Those aren't ghosts," he tried convincing himself.

He made two more right left combination turns and saw a ray of light ahead. Seeing the ray of light he also heard, "Hello." The word was followed by what he thought was a girl's laugh. He could see there was nothing ahead of him in the tunnel except the ray of light. More than curious, he went to the opening in the tunnel and stood to the side of the opening, staying out of the light. To his right he noticed more light coming in; this spilling out onto the rocky ground. The opening looked almost big enough to crawl through. He was about to take a look around the opening in front of him where the ray of light was coming from and he remembered Dutch's warning about being careful. Inching forward he could see outside, but not for long. The light blinded him. He rubbed at his eyes and leaned forward for another look.

"Hello," said a voice, the word sounding like it was being yelled back at him when he had first started playing with echoes.

Riley almost jumped out of his skin. Then he heard the giggle and he knew it came from a girl. His mind shot out a million questions all starting with the letter W. He didn't move a muscle. Then he heard the word again only this time it belonged to man's voice; perhaps a boy. Slowly he moved forward, his progress in inches. Curiosity had him ignoring caution and he looked out the slit in the wall. Without thinking, he called out, "Hello."

Chapter 9

Riley saw the source of the 'Hello echo' and the giggles. Two people about his age were standing below him surrounded by a small circle created by giant boulders. They were dressed differently than both he and Dutch. He slowly and silently wormed his way out of the cave and found himself on a ledge no bigger than he was and about eight feet above the ground. He was on his knees looking down at the strange duo. They didn't see him.

He had knelt in silence peering down at the two feeling like he was an intruder. There was another giggle and Riley was now convinced that one of the two had to be a girl. He was at a loss as to what to do. His mind kept hearing Dutch's warnings and he knew that he should stay down and slip back into tunnel opening before he gave away the entrance to the mine. Another part of him was telling him to introduce himself to the two new people. "What if I scare them?" he thought. "What if they attack me?" His mind was racing. "The ghosts aren't going to protect me now. I'm outside the mine and nowhere near the Heart." He could feel the rough ground dig into his knees. "Besides, I'm up here and they're down there. They can't get up here; I think. And, that's too far of a jump down for me to get to them." He gave his shoulders a brave shrug, stood up and showed himself to the two trespassers as he thought Dutch would've called them. They didn't notice him at first. Then, before he realized, he formed his hands into a cup and put them to his mouth. "Hello!" he yelled out.

The two young people turned and stumbled backwards; the smaller of the two's hands covering up their face.

"I'm sorry," said Riley, feeling stupid for scaring the two. He looked around frantically for a way to get down to join them. He saw he was too high up to jump and he shuffled around the edge feeling hopeless. Then, for lack of anything else to do, he said, pointing at himself, "Riley."

One set of hands uncovered a pretty face highlighted by rich, brown eyes and a smile of glistening white teeth that reflected the sun. They were both dressed in soiled white tops that resembled the medical scrubs that some of Riley's friends wore at home; a teenage fad that had kids clamoring to stores. Equally soiled white pants finished their attire that also included sandals and wide brimmed straw hats. Riley thought for a moment wondering what to do next.

The two young people looked up at Riley then unlocked their protective hug. Both of their deeply tanned faces looked back at him from under their straw hats. Their expressions made Riley think that he was a ghost. He heard the shorter one, who was a girl about his age, say something in what he knew was Spanish to her older companion.

Riley didn't know what to do so he gave a friendly wave and said, "Buenos Dias." He saw a silent question come to each face. Not knowing what else to do he pointed at himself and stated in the only other Spanish he remembered from his class at St. Pricilla's School, "Mi nombre es, Riley."

His statement received the same two identical silent questions; each face looking more puzzled than surprised. He smiled and waved again. Looking down he caught a glimpse of a second ledge slightly below where he was standing. A closer look showed a series of rock outcroppings that formed what looked like a ladder leading to the floor below. He didn't waste another second. His hiking boots navigated the rocks, and he was walking toward the two young people.

The girl, who was about his age, giggled and turned hiding her blushing face. Even though she was wearing a straw hat he could see that she had black hair that seemed to glow. Before she giggled, turned and hid her face, Riley could tell she was pretty. He could see that the boy she was with was older by a couple of years. Surprising Riley, the boy pointed at himself and said, what sounded to Riley like two words—"Hey, Zeus."

Riley vaguely knew anything about Greek gods, but repeated what he heard as a question. "Hey, Zeus? Me Riley." He then pointed at the girl who still had her face turned away from him.

"Guadalupe," said the boy.

"Gua-da-lu-pay," repeated Riley, using a phonetic pronunciation.

The boy pointed to the ledge where Riley was standing. His finger traced the path where Riley had climbed down. "Mina?" he asked.

Riley traced the boy's eyes and knew he was looking up at his trail back to the tunnel opening which was hidden by the twisting of the big rocks that formed that side of the mountain. Then he gave a timid look to the two strangers, nodded and said silently, "I'm sorry, Dutch."

The three of them heard what sounded like a rumble coming from inside the mountain. Guadalupe almost crashed into her brother as her arms wrapped around him. Her brother had a concerned look on his face; his brave front gone. Riley glanced up at where the mine's opening was hidden and mumbled, "Don't get mad at me, guys, I'm not going to give away your secret."

Riley walked up to Jesus, stuck out his hand and said, "Hi."

Without hesitation, Jesus shook his hand. Guadalupe blushed, put her hands to her face and gave a slight bend at the waist.

At first, the difference in languages caused some frustration. That quickly turned to laughter, the shaking of heads back and forth, up and down and lots of finger pointing. The three young people found themselves facing one another as they sat on large rocks trying to understand what the other was trying to convey. Many of the words came easy.

Name and Nombre; Home and Casa were easy. Live and vivir coupled with where and donde caused lots of hand gestures and imitating. Mine and mina; miners and mineros; soldiers and solados came quickly in their initial conversation. Cavalry and caballeria was made easy with Riley pretending to ride a horse. Much laughter accompanied the various translations that continued on. Family and familia; old man (referring to Dutch) and anciano was picked up quickly by the trio. The translation for Dutch was harder until El Holander' registered with Riley as a word that helped get the old man's name across to the others.

Amigo was grabbed by Riley immediately. Indians and Indios caused no problem. Neither did Apaches. That name brought on looks of fear from Jesus and Guadalupe. Riley nodded his agreement. He wanted to tell them what happened to him the night before but knew better.

Their conversation changed to more finger pointing with Jesus and Guadalupe interested in the clothing Riley wore. His t-shirt got most of the attention with both brother and sister bending close to the shirt and saying, "Serpente." Riley smiled and repeated, "Snake; a Diamondback." There was no confusion there. Riley didn't have any questions about what the brother and sister wore. Plain, white long sleeve pullovers made of a light material; their matching trousers the same along with their somewhat weather beaten, wide brim straw hats and their scuffed leather sandals knotted laces.

Riley tried to steer the conversation in the direction of why Jesus and Guadalupe were close to the mine that Dutch had managed to protect and keep a secret. There was more pointing. They tried to interpret and visualize three loud booms that they had heard while helping their family members work another mine a couple of miles to the south of where Riley found himself with Dutch. Eventually booms transposed into the evil spirits and ghosts who guarded the long sought after mine and masking any evidence of an entry to the rumored wealth and riches that lay inside. That was the explanation that Jesus and Guadalupe conveyed to Riley, the warnings they heard discussed by their elders.

Evil spirits were entrenched in the mountain from where Riley appeared. Jesus tried to explain that to Riley, but the language difference muddied the translation. At first, Jesus and Guadalupe thought that Riley was an evil spirit. Guadalupe, especially, had shown her fear of Riley's appearance and his saying, hello which, to her, sounded like, Boo. Somehow, they managed to get their sides of the story communicated; neither of the trio making fun of the other or showing any anger. When the conversation shifted back to the Caballeria and the Apaches they had no trouble communicating their feelings and showing looks of fear. Riley did not tell them about digging a grave for the three soldiers the ghosts had killed. He did elaborate as best he could as to how Dutch had explained to him about the ghosts protecting him and the old man from evil spirits. He made a loud, "Boom," to illustrate his point. Two other, "Booms," followed. Jesus and Guadalupe gave him skeptical looks. Suddenly the three of them almost turned to solid rock. The only thing moving were three sets of eyes to the right where the noise of horse's hoofs came from. Two straw hats were removed and the three of them slowly squatted down behind the rocks. They were on their hands and knees listening, not speaking, not even moving. They could hear voices, but didn't understand the language. There was no need to. It was Apache.

Riley, Jesus and Guadalupe knelt and listened for what seemed like an eternity to them. The clomping of the hoofs was barely audible. The Indians apparently were in no hurry. Sometimes the hoof beats stopped all together. How many Apaches there were they had no idea. They were relieved when they heard a few whispered words and the hoof beats start up. Riley knew what the others didn't. He was convinced the intruders were looking for the entrance to the mine. Jesus and Guadalupe weren't but, then again, he thought, maybe they were, sent to find the mine by their elders. Riley didn't know what to think. One thing he didn't want to experience again was a hand around his neck; the hand of someone who wanted to kill him.

The sound of the horses had moved off, but the trio knelt still. It was Jesus who slowly raised his right hand and put his index finger to his lips. Riley's head barely moved to acknowledge the sign. Guadalupe's shy eyes had turned deathly serious. She gave a nod.

They waited on hands and knees continuing to listen. The air was still, the sky minus a solitary soaring bird, no sounds of a far-off coyote. They kept listening. Nothing moved. At one point, Jesus put his ear to the ground and Riley followed his action. They only heard the sound of coarse sand brushing into their ear canals. Jesus began to slowly crawl forward keeping out of sight until he came to a break in the rock cover. He peered around the corner and quickly pulled back, his face telling the others what they didn't want to know.

What he saw was an Indian inching his way in their direction, the Indian's head and eyes slowly and carefully scanning and searching. When he saw the Indian the Indian, he felt, didn't see him. At least he thought that and hoped he was right.

At first thought, Riley felt the fear of being trapped again; the vice-like grip around his neck ready to send him to the pale face's Happy Hunting Ground. His mind whirled and he tried to remember all of the places Dutch had told him about, the escape routes. There were the dead ends, the dangerous drop offs and Das Chute. In a short time he had learned most of the tunnels in the mine. He knew that if they could get inside without being seen they would be safe. He was reassured by the fact that Dutch had promised him the mine's ghosts would protect him. Riley got off his knees and rolled over to where he was sitting down. His back was resting up against a large rock along with his head. He traced the rock formations to his left and then to his right looking for a familiar landmark, a clue to a path leading to safety. There was none. "Doggone," he said silently. He closed his eyes and thought. In the next instant his eyes popped open when he felt a nudge against his arm. It was Jesus. Guadalupe was at his side; both of them still on their hands and knees. Jesus gave him a reassuring nod and then indicated with his head that Riley should follow him and his sister. Riley didn't ask and rolled quietly to his hands and knees.

Jesus led them through a series of curved openings in the rocks that was an angle to the right and away from the Indian. They found themselves in a large circular opening big enough for the three of them to stretch out. Jesus indicated with his finger to stay put. Riley and Guadalupe watched him crawl back on the route they had taken. After about fifteen minutes, both Riley and Guadalupe started to show their concern by communicating with their eyes. Their eyes showed concern coated with fear. Just then, Jesus returned.

In a whisper, Jesus said, "I went back to wipe away any trace of where we had crawled. His hushed explanation in Spanish was accompanied by a set of hand gestures Riley understood. They each brushed at their knees, Riley especially since his were bare. He sat with his back against a rock again and repeated his search of their surroundings looking for something familiar. His eyes went left and he saw nothing he recognized. Then his eyes traveled right; again nothing. A feeling of depression began to close in on him. "Doggone," he muttered. He sighed and then his heart almost caused the rattles on his Diamondback t-shirt to start vibrating. He was staring at Das Chute.

Chapter 10

Luck and ghosts protecting them from evil spirits and, in this case, a stalking Indian who had stayed behind to surprise them, was not how the three young people had intended to spend their day.

Jesus and Guadalupe had been sent out by their extended family to see if they could find the source of the three loud booms that had echoed across the valley the night before. According to Jesus who had said to Riley by use of finger pointing and a variety of hand gestures, "My Tia Maria, who sleeps like a rock, was awaken by the three loud explosions."

Riley felt more confused than ever. He had two new friends. There was Dutch. His feelings didn't make sense, and he was convinced that no one in his family would believe what he had experienced. William wouldn't. "He'd think I've gone looney after I tell him about burying three cavalry soldiers that included and Indian scout." Now he was about to be attacked by Apaches.

The three young people wondered if they could find a safe haven to keep clear of the Indian who seemed to know where they were going before they did. This time it was Riley who led the way. His silent instruction to Jesus, with a series of sweeping motions with his palm, was to erase any signs of their route from their pursuer.

The course was narrow and tight; way too tight for an adult

body to pass through, but the three young people made their way on their hands and knees. Riley would stop momentarily, take a look up to get his bearings, and then lead the other two. All the while he kept wondering if he was doing the right thing. Would Dutch be upset with him for bringing strangers into his secret gold mine? Even worse, he was showing them the way in. But he believed that Dutch wouldn't be upset from saving his two new friends and himself from possible mayhem.

Riley made one more rest stop, brushed at his knees that were now raw, both sporting blisters, one showing a trickle of blood. Now, for the first time, he began to doubt if he had actually seen Das Chute and if they were going in the right direction. He indicated that they should start up again. Jesus and Guadalupe resumed following him without any sign of hesitation or doubt. None of them made a sound.

They had only crawled for about a minute when they came upon a turn in the rocks. Then he saw it. He was looking at the pile of rocks that covered the grave he had dug with Dutch. Riley barely exhaled a sigh of relief. He knew they would be safe now. In minutes they would be inside the opening in the tunnel leading them to the Heart. No one, not even an Indian, would be able to follow them and find the way into the entrance of the Lost Dutchman.

Jesus and Guadalupe couldn't believe where they were standing. They rattled off in Spanish their feelings way too fast for Riley to understand. Had Riley known their excitement exceeded being safe he might have changed his mind about getting them to safety. What Riley didn't realize was why the brother and sister were as close to Dutch's mine as they were. Limited Spanish and plenty of hand gestures had him kind of understanding that they had been sent out by family members to find the source of the explosions echoing across the valley in the middle of the night. Rumors of an old miner who had discovered the mother lode were not new and not limited to a few prospectors, the greedy and the unscrupulous who would do anything to become rich. Almost everyone had heard the stories about the mine where the mother lode was located. Some scoffed when hearing tales of the mine being haunted and guarded over by a crazy old man who believed in evil spirits. The crazy old man also protected himself with a large rifle rumored to have been used to kill mammoth animals in a far off place called Deutschland. If the brother and sister could find a trail to that mine, there were enough family members along with arms and ammunition to take care of a crazy old man even if he did have a rifle rumored to shoot through rocks, even if he had evil spirits protecting him. So they thought.

Riley didn't hesitate. Jesus and Guadalupe so close to him they were almost riding his back. Inside the mine opening they sat in the shadows. Both Riley and Jesus carefully peered around the protective cover of the rocks forming the slime entrance. They saw nothing. Without a word they both knew what they had to do. Jesus followed Riley back along the tight, twisting elevated trail until the trail branched off in several directions. Then, working as a team, each got down on his hands and knees and started back to the mine opening using their hands to sweep away their tracks and any evidence they, or anyone else, had been there.

Back inside the mine, Guadalupe hugged her brother. Riley didn't stop. He stood up and motioned for the other two to follow him in silence. His fear seemed to disappear even though he knew they might still be in danger. That is, if the Indian who had be stalking them was wearing a Kepi.

After leading Jesus and Guadalupe through the tunnel and up into the mountain, he stopped at a familiar place where a ray of light streamed through the opening and looked out. "God," he muttered, so his two companions heard him.

"Dios?" questioned Jesus, his sister's eyes asking the same question.

Riley stepped aside and pointed to the opening. Jesus carefully positioned his head and looked out. He jumped back and whispered, "Madre."

"How did he know where we were going?" asked Riley, using his hands and shoulders to convey his question to Jesus and Guadalupe. There wasn't much translation needed. Apaches knew how to track, and this one was especially good at tracking. Hand palms wiping up a trail only made for a trail that stuck out more than Riley's blistered bleeding knees. It was as if Riley, Jesus and Guadalupe had stood up and waved for the Indian to join them.

Riley took another look out the opening. He could see the Indian, but the Indian, so he thought, couldn't see him. He pulled back and said, "He's still coming." He didn't bother to use any type of sign language. He didn't have to. Both brother and sister knew. Riley's mind was once again whirling. It stopped long enough when he indicated that his companions should follow him. When they got to the opening of Das Chute,

Riley spelled out his plan the best he could. The Indian would surely find the opening to the mine and would have no trouble tracking them to the end of the tunnel to where the opening of Das Chute was. At least he wouldn't be led to the Heart. His plan was simple and based on the fact that there were three of them and only one Indian. Guadalupe would be the decoy. The two boys, each armed with a long handle shovel, would be on each side of the tunnel. When the Indian would go for Guadalupe either one or both would get him with their shovel. It would be easy.

It wasn't.

It didn't take the Indian tracker long to find them. His speed and efficiency surprised the three. They had no sooner formulated and rehearsed their plan when they heard a faint noise in the tunnel. A small pebble had been uncharacteristically disturbed. They quickly got in position, Guadalupe sitting in a ray of sunshine as if she were a blessed icon in a Mexican village church. Riley and Jesus stood totally still clutching their shovels in the darkness to either side of the entrance leading to Das Chute.

The Indian never stopped. What he did do that Riley and Jesus didn't expect was that he dropped to a squat when entering the darkness, knowing or sensing that his prey had turned into predators. His senses were right on as both boys swung their shovels as hard as they could. Both swinging shovels clanged together with terrific force knocking them from the boys' hands. They quickly returned to being the prey.

Guadalupe let out a scream as both Riley and Jesus dropped

to their knees and groped for the shovel handles. The Indian beat them. One shovel got kicked to the side while the other cracked Riley on his shoulder sending him against the rock wall knocking the wind from him. He dropped to the ground. The Indian then stalked Jesus who was in a crouched position circling the Indian and keeping his distance as best he could. When the Indian was in the sunlight all three of the young people could see that he was smiling. The sunlight also flashed off what looked like a knife blade in his hand; a rather large knife and one bigger than they had ever seen. Even Dutch's knife looked small by comparison.

Jesus continued circling the Indian until he was in front of Guadalupe who hadn't moved. She was trembling, her hands clasped in prayer. Jesus muttered something to her in Spanish and positioned his body in front of her and the Indian. Like a cat, the Indian was on Jesus, one hand on his pullover and the other hand ready to strike with the knife. Guadalupe managed a scream before she and her brother heard the crack of a solid object against bone. The Indian crumbled to the ground.

Riley had recovered enough to find the shovel that the Indian kicked away. It didn't take him long, knowing the layout of the tunnel and the opening to Das Chute, to surprise the Indian. He hit him across the back of the skull and knocked him down. The knife fell at the feet of Guadalupe who quickly picked it up. There was another crack of the shovel and the three of them looked down upon either a very unconscious Indian or a lifeless one. Riley wasted no time in grabbing the assailant by the heels; the maneuver now seeming like a habit. He began pulling, almost yelling to Jesus, "Help me get this guy to the opening." Then he found himself holding on to one ankle for dear life, the other leg knocking his legs out from under him. The Indian most certainly wasn't dead, but Riley now had visions of his own demise. Being chased the night before and running for his life wasn't quickly forgotten. In an instant he felt both of the Indian's hands around his throat and his entire body being lifted off the tunnel's dirt floor. The Indian let out a scream and Riley prepared himself to be thrown through the air like a human spear to be stuck in the rock wall head first. Then they heard a loud explosion and he felt the Indian's hands loosen from his neck. His feet came in contact with the dirt floor. As if in slow motion the Indian crumbled face first to the ground. Riley glanced at Guadalupe who was shaking. The sun's rays were shining brightly off the handle of the Indian's knife that was still in her hand; the blade clean. The knife slowly slipped from her hands falling to the ground. Guadalupe sat wringing her hands while gasping on her tears. She couldn't speak.

Jesus had crawled over to his sister and gently picked up the knife and held it in his left hand, his rights stroking his sister's quivering shoulders. Both of his arms slowly went around her and he hugged her close for the longest time while stroking her hair. Neither said a word.

Riley stepped over the Indian and looked carefully out of the opening. "God," he said again, his one word sounding hopeless.

As Jesus and Guadalupe looked at him they seemed to know. The Indian party had stopped riding off in their decoying action and had returned to pick up their other member and, who they thought, would be prisoners. Riley took another look and could see the horses clustered together in one of the natural circular corrals made by the rock formations. The party was wasting no time scampering through the rock crevices, sometimes seeming to glide over them like the tiny dessert lizards he had seen with his grandfather. "Gosh, they're fast," he remembered saying to his grandfather.

Riley recalled from the night before with Dutch that there was one area where the Indians would have to slow down. He waved his hand at his companions signaling them to follow him down a tunnel that he had explored before. In moments, they were beside the rock wall that had the two openings; one vertical and the other round. The round hole was situated at the bottom of the wall. He grabbed a large rock with both hands. It was so heavy Riley could barely lift it. He placed it by the large circular hole in the wall. It looked like it would just fit through the opening. He signaled to Jesus and Guadalupe to do the same thing. He helped Guadalupe while her brother seemed to have no trouble carrying his rock. They repeated the process until there were six rocks lined up at the hole.

Riley signaled for Jesus to join him looking out the vertical opening. Without saying a word, he pointed to a spot that was directly below the circular hole. Above and to both sides of the hole were piles of rock, big rock, balancing, in many cases on top of each other. Below that was the trail leading up to them. Coming up the trail were the Indians. Riley gave a series of hand signals and gestures that Jesus understood right away.

When their assailants were stacked up single file on the trail with only two ways to go, up or down, and the footing even precarious for a lizard, Jesus was to shove a rock into and through the hole. Guadalupe, sitting down, was to use her feet and legs to push the rock through sending it down on the pursuers. As fast as she could push a rock through the opening, Jesus and Riley would roll in another one. They could only hope the plan to cause a rock slide would work. They were out of options.

As soon as Riley had given Jesus and Guadalupe the signal, he dashed over to help them. The first rock, the biggest, had jammed in the opening. Three sets of strong legs pushed and the rock went hurling downward toward the unsuspecting trackers. The three young people didn't know that the other rocks wouldn't be necessary. The first rock created a massive rock slide that sent tons of the mountain on the assailants. Riley, Jesus and Guadalupe kept rolling, shoving and kicking the other rocks through the opening, the clatter of the falling rocks resembling the thunder that Riley had experienced the night before and what they had heard earlier that saved them from annihilation.

Riley went back to the vertical opening and looked down. "Wow," he stated. He looked for several seconds and then stepped aside to let Jesus and Guadalupe take a look. They both turned to look at Riley, their eyes growing bigger, a smile forming on the face of Jesus. Guadalupe's brown eyes reflected awe.

"Come on," said Riley, as he turned at headed back to Das Chute. He hurried along knowing that there was a body that needed to be removed before Dutch returned. He dashed to the end of the tunnel, stopped, turned around, looked and then felt his heart drop down to the pit of his stomach. The Indian had vanished.

Riley slowly turned expecting to once again come face-to-face with his nemesis. He saw nothing. Unbelieving, he started for the Das Chute opening and tripped on something. It was the knife. He looked down and picked it up. He cautiously looked out the opening of Das Chute and saw the Indian sprawled atop the grave of the three he and Dutch had buried. He was on his back, arms extended up, one hand clenched as if it were reaching for the sky. "He's pointing at the Happy Hunting Ground," he muttered. What scared Riley was that the Indian's eyes were open as if staring at Riley; a look of fear etched in the once proud face.

After Jesus and Guadalupe had a look, Guadalupe's reluctance brought on no more than a glimpse, they knew what they had to do. Riley would show them the way down and there would be one more soul to add to the rock grave; that soul joining the others on their way to the Happy Hunting Ground.

Chapter 11

The burial was quick yet dignified and respectful. There were plenty of rocks from the slide and digging wasn't necessary. Riley even took the time at the end to mutter a part of what he remembered from Dutch's prayer about ashes to ashes. "Amen," he said at the end and made a Sign of the Cross. He noticed Jesus and Guadalupe do the same thing.

After a series of hand gestures and frustrated language translations, they decided to take the Indian ponies and ride them back to the other mine where Jesus and Guadalupe could rejoin their family. Riley didn't want to be alone in the Heart after their experience, and he decided to ride with them. He had never been on a horse before and it didn't take Jesus and Guadalupe long before their laughter echoed across the valley as they watched him wrap his arms around the pony's neck in a bear hug. The cowboys riding horses in the western movies he saw on television made it look easy. They barely bounced up and down. He did more than bounce almost falling off with every beat of his pony's hoofs. His arms held onto the horse's neck harder than the Indian assailant from the U.S. Cavalry who lifted him off the ground and almost choked the life out of him.

The ponies clomped along at a pace not much faster than a walk. After a while, Riley let loose of the strangle hold on the pony's neck and sat up like the others. He was still unsure of what to do if the pony decided to break out into a gallop, but he tried to do what his two companions in front of him did, and his confidence slowly grew along with the soreness between his legs that added to the pain he felt from his bleeding knees.

Eventually, the three of them were riding side by side, the language difference no longer seeming to be a barrier. Hand and even facial gestures overcame the meaning of words. They laughed, at least Jesus and Riley did. Guadalupe only smiled and most of that done with her dark eyes that both intrigued and told Riley she liked him. Cowboys in his television movies didn't have girlfriends, but he didn't care. He had never had a real girlfriend either, but he thought Guadalupe would be the only girl he would ever want to know.

Most of their laughter was directed at the mishaps of their encounters with the Indians. The clanging of their shovels and the pushing and shoving of the rocks that created the rock slide and trapped the Indians had ended their chance to capture the three young people. Their topic of conversation quickly changed to an old blind man who lived alone. He was known as Blind Charlie, "Carlos," said Jesus as he covered his eyes with both hands.

Riley's reply was to squint and then cover his own eyes with both hands and repeating what Jesus had said. "He's blind?" asked Riley, wondering how anyone could survive in the desert without being able to see.

Blind Charlie's ranch was situated between the mine where the families of Jesus and Guadalupe worked and the border of Mexico. Riley, with lots of help and patience from his two Mexican friends, managed to deduce that the man named Charlie who was not only blind, but was said to possess, according to Jesus, "Magia fuerte." Riley quickly picked up on the magic part of the folklore and, with Jesus flexing his biceps, got the message that Blind Charlie was indeed strong and not one to mess with.

Blind Charlie lived on the ranch that the Mexicans and Apaches had dubbed, Mal Casa. Riley had no problem with the word, casa, but he became frustrated with trying to translate the Spanish for evil. He went through bad, wicked, nasty, ugly, haunted and two dozen other names before, his frustration level was at a boiling point and he shouted out, "That old guy's house is just plain evil."

Jesus clapped his hands and said, "Si. Evil."

Riley learned that Blind Charlie's ranch was avoided by Indians, some of the Mexican miners and even some travelers had heard stories about Blind Charlie and his evil ranch house. It seems that the Dutchman and his mountain weren't the only ones in the Sonoran Desert who possessed supernatural powers and were often looked upon as not human. Satan and devil were two terms bandied about, but the most frequent description was El Diablo. Riley didn't know about Blind Charlie, but he did know about his friend, Dutch, and there had been growing doubts running through his brain concerning him. There were too many events explained by Dutch that Riley couldn't fathom. Now he was hearing more unbelievable stories about a man named Blind Charlie. Then there was El Diablo. Riley didn't want to believe what he was thinking, but his thoughts about Dutch were throwing up questions. Those questions related to what he had been taught in religion classes during his years at St. Pricilla's School.

Riley sat on his pony in front of the entrance to the mine where the families and friends of Jesus and Guadalupe surrounded the two youngsters almost burying them with hugs and kisses. Their attention soon switched to Riley.

Spanish flew out of his companions and their family, mostly from the family directed at Riley who managed to understand only a couple of words, those related to who and where. He didn't need a translator or hand gestures with Jesus and Guadalupe to spell out what some of the adults gathered around their mine's entrance were thinking. "Oh, oh," he thought while forcing a smile.

Two of the older men, their clothing stained from sweat and dirt approached Riley. His pony let out a slight noise, his mouth and lips seeming to flap while a hoof gave one faint paw at the ground. Riley took a guess, nodded at the nearest of the two men and asked, Padre?" His guess was right and the tension that seemed evident coming from the man seemed to vanish.

The other man, as Jesus quickly pointed out, was introduced as Tio Poncho, the uncle of Jesus and Guadalupe. The uncle's tension had also left, but his eyes couldn't hide what was on his mind, and Riley suddenly realized that he was about to be leading a part, or even all, of the Mexican family and miners to Dutch's Heart. He glanced at Jesus and Guadalupe. There was a look that said, "Thank you, amigo for saving our lives," and another one that followed with the shifting of their eyes in a direction he should make his exit. Their look was coated with fear and a second message that said, "Forgive us, amigo." More of the miners, about a dozen in number, had congregated outside the mine entrance and had started to walk slowly toward Riley.

Riley's hands went slowly to the pony's mane where he gently stroked and patted the animal's neck. He glanced at the father of his two friends then looked at the brother and sister and gave a warm smile. He glanced at their father who had joined the other menacing group getting nearer to him. Riley saw their father's eyes were no longer showing any signs of a smile. "Buena tarde," said Riley, using one of the few expressions he had learned in his grammar school Spanish class. He glanced back to Jesus and Guadalupe who grasped their straw hats in their right hands. Their eyes said all that had to be said. The final message was, "Vaya con Dios." Then they let out a yell, their straw hats slapping at their thighs while another yell followed. At the same time, Riley's hands clutched the pony's mane as his legs squeezed and kicked the sides of the pony. The horse shot forward making Riley feel like he was watching a televised horse race. He was hanging on for all he was worth as the horse quickly put distance between the miners and his two friends. There was no looking back even though he wanted to wave good-bye to his two new friends. Waving would have him being thrown from the galloping horse and in the hands of the miners. Had he looked back he would've seen that Jesus and Guadalupe had their arms around the necks of the pony's detaining anyone from trying to take their horses and pursuing Riley. Family members tried to pull them loose but neither of the youngsters would let go. Had Riley heard what they were shouting his feelings about fleeing for his life wouldn't have been as great. The brother and sister were screaming. Guadalupe's screams were filled with tears, as they tried to tell the others that Riley had risked his life to save them from a small band of Apaches. Jesus and Guadalupe continued to hang onto their ponies as if they possessed a super human strength that surprised those who were doing the pulling and tugging. The longer they held on to the ponies, the farther Riley got and the smaller his size became on the horizon until the only thing visible was a faint trail of dust.

Riley rode the horse at full gallop until he thought his hands and legs could no longer squeeze any harder. He had no idea where he was going or what he was doing but he let up on his pressures and the pony slowed down and seemed to thank him by shaking his head up and down several times. Only then did Riley turn around to see if anyone was chasing him from the mine. There was nothing but barren desert behind him. He looked ahead and saw a faint sign of smoke. "Not more Indians," he muttered, as his head went back and forth and his hopes for being with his family again seemed to vanish like the faint sign of smoke he now tried to use as a beacon.

The pony clomped slowly along heading for the smoke as if no direction was being given by his rider. Riley could make out a small house and what looked like a corral. He saw several native trees, a couple he recognized as Palo Verdes that grew on his grandfather's property. "I bet this must be Blind Charlie's ranch," he said to his pony.

The horse's head went up and down a couple of times as he continued toward the house. As he got closer, he could make out a person walking along the outside of the corral, a hand tracing the corral fence rail never losing touch. As the pony got closer Riley had to do a double take. The man he saw looked like Dutch, red suspenders included. A million questions raced through him. One of them: Should he continue to the ranch or get his pony heading in another direction? He didn't wait long for his answer.

Riley knew in an instant what he would do. A cloud of dust surrounding a half dozen galloping horses made his decision easier. What added to his easy decision was the fact that the six horses were being ridden by an equal number of very vocal Apaches.

Riley let out a yelp and his heels kicked into the horse's flanks. His horse bolted so fast and so hard that Riley almost flew off the back. Grabbing his horse's mane for all he was worth, Riley headed for the corral. He could see the old man feeling his way up the wooden steps of his ranch house. "Dutch!" yelled Riley. "Dutch, it's der Bub!" He could see the old man look in his direction. Riley gave a quick, frantic wave and latched onto the horse's mane again as he rode under the log arch that had three "X's" made out of parts of tree branches hanging from it by what looked like leather lanyards. Riley's panic increased as he heard the hoof beats of the Indians' horses along with their yells and yelps. "Help me, Dutch!" he hollered.

The grizzled looking old man stood on the porch holding on to one of the log supports holding up the roof. He waved at Riley, but never said a word.

Riley found himself surrounded in dust, horses and Indians as he got off his own horse. Hands grabbed at him. He shook them off. More hands grabbed and he stumbled to the ground. Crawling as fast as he could, he scooted around a pair of moccasins; then he was between a pair of them. He felt another jam down on his back, but he kept going. From hands and knees he went to hands and toes; his speed gaining. His right hand hit the first wooden step of the porch; his left landed on the second. Up he scampered. Both hands were on the porch deck; his right foot joining his hands. His left foot didn't make it. A quick glance over his shoulder and he was looking into an Indian's painted face. The Indian was not happy. Riley didn't waste a second. "If at first you don't succeed," he blurted out, "try, try..." He recalled his grandfather's instructions about what to do if attacked. It had worked once, maybe it would work again. He twisted ending up between the Indian's legs. His free leg shot out and made a solid contact with something. The something turned out to be a very surprised Indian. There was the predicted whoosh and the moan. His leg was free and Riley sprung up landing on the porch where he promptly ran into a pair of red suspenders. A pair of hands grabbed him by the shoulders, turned him and pushed him through the open door of the ranch house. He tripped and ended up on the floor as he heard a pair of boots shuffle behind him and then a door was slammed shut.

"What in tar nation are you tryin' to do, Lad," get me killed.

"Dutch?" Riley managed to blurb out.

"Who in the dickens is Dutch?" the voice asked.

Riley looked up from his position on the floor and stared into a pair of eyes that didn't stare back. They couldn't stare. The old man was blind. "I'm sorry, Sir," he said, sounding out of breath. The sound of pounding on the door and the commotion on the porch had him standing and holding onto the old man's shoulders. "I thought you were somebody I knew.

He lives in the Superstitions."

"Oh, that Dutch," said the old man.

Riley noticed the pounding and the commotion outside had subsided and he peered over the old man's shoulders at the front door.

"Looks like those crazy devils are going away," said the old man.

"Really," said Riley, hearing the sounds of horses' hooves slowly as three thuds hit the side of the house in succession.

"Gall dang arrows," said the old man.

"Why'd they shoot arrows at your house, sir?" asked Riley. "Why didn't they just break down the door? There were enough of them and only two of us."

The old man slowly turned Riley around so that he was in front of him. His blank eyes looked down at Riley. "Kind of short and young to be running around alone in these parts," he said. "Ain't very smart either."

Riley didn't know what to say. He kept quiet and felt his breathing return to normal. "So, why did those Apaches shoot arrows into your house?" he asked.

"Like I just said, Lad, you ain't too smart." The old man grinned. "I reckon you haven't heard that you're in the evil house of El Diablo, have you?"

"I didn't know, Sir," said Riley. "But, I did hear about the evil house and El Diablo." He paused and asked politely: "Are you the man they call Blind Charlie?"

The man laughed. "The one and only, Lad," he said, another laugh followed. "And what are you known by?"

"Riley," the old man repeated. "Ain't never known no Riley before, but you're welcome here," he said. "And, safe too," he continued. "Safe just as long as those Injuns think I possess medicine stronger than they have."

"I sure hope so, Sir."

The old man's head gave a slight jerk up and his right index finger went to his lips while his left hand slid clumsily down Riley's face covering his mouth.

Riley stood like one of the rocks that he remembered guarded the entrance to Dutch's mine. He thought he heard the creak of a board on the porch and he could see the old man's head nod ever so slightly. Then the old man turned, reached out behind him and started to move across the room in a strange fashion. Riley noticed the old man take three long strides and stop. Then the old man slid his right foot to the right and tapped his toe. His right foot moved again; this time to the left. There was another toe tap. That was followed by the right foot moving on a diagonal to the right. This time the toe tap produced a hollow sound. The old man pointed and indicated that Riley should get down on the floor and look for a loose floor board.

Riley knew right away what the old man wanted him to do. He found the loose boards without having to search. The boards were pulled up and put off to the side of an opening that was big enough for a body to get through. Riley saw a hand waving in his face and he grabbed it. The old man moved like a feather floating down from the side of the Superstitions. He was in the opening in the floor; the bottom of his suspenders just hidden by the boards. He nodded his head indicating that Riley should get into the opening. As Riley's feet hit solid ground, the old man pushed his head under the floor boards. Riley heard a slight scrapping, and the old man had replaced the boards. No evidence of light could be seen. The old man touched Riley's right ear and he bent forward and whispered.

"Old Indian trick," he said. "One of them takes all the horses and rides off leaving the others behind. He ain't gone very far. Them there others are out in the corral flashing signals and making plans to get us. Looks like this bunch don't believe in the evil magic this old blind man is supposed to possess," he said, catching his breath. "Hood winked them for a long time."

Riley's ears strained to hear, but there wasn't a sound coming from above or anywhere else. "Charlie, Sir," he whispered. "What do we do now?" Then he smelled smoke. Blind Charlie's house was on fire.

Chapter 12

Riley and Charlie had carefully crawled through the gagging and eye burning smoke under the house to where the front steps led up to the porch. They didn't make a sound. Charlie led the way as if he had perfect vision. In his mind, and the limited world of his ranch and house, he did. Neither of them needed perfect vision when they first saw the patient moccasins lined up at the back of the house. Riley's heart had taken a nose dive and sank to the bottom of his stomach. He wanted to know what the old man was planning to do, but Blind Charlie had anticipated Riley's question and held his index finger to his lips. Riley, his bare knees back to getting beat up by desert rock and sand, crouched along side of the old man and stayed silent. He watched the old man who was listening intently, blank eyes staring straight ahead.

Charlie knew what was happening long before Riley smelled the smoke. The blind man's senses honed in on the sound of a flint being struck. Riley had heard the noise too, but didn't know what it was and why the Indians were doing what they were doing.

The old, dry wooden boards of the porch ignited as if gasoline had been poured on them. There was no gas only some small hand rolled balls of straw from the dilapidated barn. The Indians were talking, their excitement growing as Charlie pointed to the back of the house where the Indian ponies were.

Then Charlie's nose wrinkled several times and he pointed in the direction where the flames were devouring the steps and said, "They plan to smoke us out."

Riley didn't need an explanation to know the Indians' plan. The fire would drive them out of the back of the house and into six pairs of waiting hands that weren't interested in greeting or saving them. Their special idea for a greeting would entertain only them. Then Riley heard Charlie whisper to him, "I heard your pony in the corral. When I give you a nudge you crawl out from under here," he said, his finger pointing to the left side of the burning steps that were almost charcoal. "Get on that horse of yours and head directly for the sun. Don't stop and don't you dare look back. Understand?"

Riley understood but he had to say what he did. "What about you, Charlie? I ain't leavin' you alone. No way," he said, his stern voice showing no signs of nerves.

Charlie raised his hand and placed it on the top of Riley's head. "Don't you go worryin' about me," he said, as the flames bore into the main part of the house and curls of smoke worked their way into the crawl space. "I'm El Diablo and this here house is evil, remember?"

"I don't care," said Riley. "You're blind and I ain't gonna leave you. No way. My grandfather and father would both kick my butt."

Charlie gave Riley another pat on the head. "You're a brave lad, Riley. But, you worry too much. I've got a surprise cooked up for our friends waiting back there," he said, a smile starting to form.

"I not leaving without you," Riley said, surprised at the feelings racing through him.

"You sure are a stubborn cuss," said the old man. "Look," he said, turning on his side to face the back of the house. "See that big wooden box sitting back there? Unless those Indians squat down and take a look they don't see it," he continued. "That box is filled with dynamite. Don't know how good it is 'cause it's kind of old; been sitting there longer than I can remember."

"Dynamite?" repeated Riley. "That's what was on the box I saw in that Disney World town of Tumbleweed before the Thunder Mountain roller coaster started out."

Blind Charlie acted as if he didn't hear a word Riley had said. "See this," he said, holding out a six shooter that had a white pearl handle and a glistening silver steel barrel.

"Is that real?" Riley asked, his eyes soaking up the weapon's shape. "Wow! Just like in the movies."

"Movies?" repeated Charlie. His hand rested on Riley's shoulder. "Now listen to me, Lad," he said. "When I give you a push you crawl out and head for the corral and your pony. I'll be right behind you. I'm gonna give you five seconds and then I'm gonna start shootin' at that box. Here's hopin' it blows the livin' kingdom come out of our friends waiting for us behind the house." Charlie paused and then said to Riley, "Before I give you that push, point my right hand in the direction of that dynamite box."

Riley, his own hand shaking, followed Charlie's orders and had the old man's hand pointing at the wooden box. He took a quick look back and, just before he turned forward, part of the floor caved in; flames and smoke going in all directions. Instinctively, he and Charlie ducked and covered their heads with their arms. Riley felt the flames on his bare legs.

"You okay, Lad?"

"I'm good."

"That's what I like to hear," said Blind Charlie. He gave Riley a shove and said, "Get!"

The Indians must have heard the voices coming from under the house. Five sets of eyes peered at Charlie, and he squeezed the trigger of his revolver. He missed the box marked Dynamite, but hit one of the marauders. A cry went up. Charlie fired another round. That one hit the box, but nothing happened. He fired again. The bullet found the box but not the explosives. "Three's a charm," said Charlie, in a normal voice. The gun went off and so did the Dynamite. The back half of the house turned into a tangled mess of flying boards covered with flames. At least five of their pursuers had disappeared. The force of the blast had blown Charlie toward the corral. Unfortunately, on his way there he went through the burning front steps of his ranch house. Fortune wasn't totally on the side of Riley either. After he heard the blast, Riley turned and saw Charlie lying face down on the ground. His heavy pants were smoldering and he wasn't moving.

"Charlie," he called out, and started to crawl to where the old man lay. As he reached the old man, he rolled him over on his back and began pulling him toward the corral. His pulling Charlie put out the smoldering trousers and started to revive him. He felt the old man's hand move and grab a hold of his. "Hang on, Charlie," he gasped. "Hang on."

That's when Riley felt a hand grab him by the hair and another hand slap him hard across the face. He heard a yell and a yelp then another yell. The hand on his hair gave a yank that almost ripped it out by the roots. His captor appeared interested in more than removing Riley's scalp. There was no tomahawk visible in his hand, and no other form of a homemade hatchet or club. What Riley saw was a knife; a knife bigger than the one Dutch used to serve up beans for dinner. He could feel himself panic and then he heard himself say, "Nah." The word came out so calmly that it startled the Indian who was ready to start his knife on a downward thrust that would be the end of Riley "Rocky" Stone. He grinned up at the warrior who was about to end his life. "Nah," he said again. Then his foot shot out like an arrow leaving a hunter's bow and jammed into the Indian's groin.

Riley couldn't believe that his grandfather's predictions came through again, but Riley wasn't interested in seeing the results of his kick. He grabbed Charlie, got up and began dragging the old man as fast as he could. In moment he was by the pony that seemed to wait dutifully for him. "Hang on, Charlie," he said to the old man, his words more like an order than a request from a young boy. He could see the Indian struggle to his feet and then go for his knife that was several yards behind him. "Come on, Charlie you're getting on this horse with me whether you want to or not." As he stood Charlie up and tried to boost the old man onto the back of the horse, he heard an explosion. "Gosh darn," he said. "That can't be Dutch and his good spirits saving me again."

It wasn't. When Charlie had ignited the dynamite, two sticks had been blown forward and out from under the house. They laid there minding their business until more of the house caved in. This time the front part of the roof and some of the burning timbers landed on the dynamite. Why the dynamite took its time exploding no one will ever know. Riley didn't care. The Indian didn't either. His days of caring had come to an end and he was on his way to the Happy Hunting Ground.

Riley got on the horse with Charlie lying in front of him. "Hang on, Charlie," he said. "We're going to be safe." The pony broke into a gallop surprising both Riley and Charlie almost throwing them from its back. Without a command the pony's nose pointed south toward the Mexican border and his gallop increased. Riley's mind felt as if another dynamite stick had exploded in his skull. "We'll be safe in Mexico, Charlie," he said, his words bouncing out of his throat in synchronization with the pony's hoofs pounding on the hard desert ground. "I know that Jesus and Guadalupe will be there to help us," he said hopefully. "Hang on, Charlie."

"Hang on!" He heard the familiar voice shout. His hand was squeezed so hard he thought that his fingers would be crushed into the fine gravel and sand from underneath Blind Charlie's house. "Hang on," the voice said again, a hint of panic visible. The voice didn't belong to Blind Charlie.

"Hang on!" came a cry, but it wasn't Riley who cried out the warning. He looked down and Blind Charlie was gone. Also gone was the galloping pony. Riley felt his left hand being squeezed and his arm almost being pulled from its socket. "I gotcha," said a labored voice. It was the voice of Riley's cousin, William. "You're safe, man," said William, trying to catch his breath. "Wow that was sure a close one."

Riley's head was spinning and his upper body ached as if he had bounced down Das Chute landing on a mountain of boulders. He saw a bright light ahead and heard the sound of clapping hands, whistling and excited shouts of joy. Just then he was blinded by daylight and he was standing still or, better yet, sitting still. Then it dawned on him. He was in a roller coaster car; the last one and seated next to his cousin who had a worried look on his face. "Boy," said William to his very confused younger cousin as he shook his head from side to side, "that's what you get for showing off and trying to stand up. You almost got tossed out of the back of this car," he continued, none too pleased with his cousin's careless behavior. "Thank God these things are designed to keep morons like you safe from acting stupid."

"Why are you calling me, stupid?" asked Riley, surprised at what his cousin was saying to him. "What did I do? What happened?"

"You almost got thrown from the car when you tried to stand up. You kept yelling about hanging on to someone called Blind Charlie. You were screaming your brains out. Then you were kicking at someone you called an Apache scout. Geez, you said he was trying to scalp you."

"I did?" asked Riley. "A real Apache?" He paused and looked sheepishly at his cousin as they exited the roller coaster car and could see the rest of his family ahead of them. "Did I say anything about Jesus?" He paused again. "Did I mention the name, Guadalupe?"

"Man, that's what you get for not eating breakfast," said William. "I ain't ever riding on a roller coaster with you again, you idiot. I had to force you down to keep from falling out of the car. You let out a howl once and I thought you hit your hand on something."

"My hands are fine," said Riley showing them to his cousin

as they joined up with the rest of the family. Before anyone could say a word, Riley was hugging his mother. His father was next. Then he surprised his sister and hugged her. She backed away and made a face before saying, "Ugh. Gross."

"You guys have fun?" asked his uncle.

"Yeah," they both responded in unison, nothing being said about the incident.

"Riley," his mother said sounding alarmed. "What happened to your knees? Why they're blistered and I see...." She stopped and looked at Riley's father. "Is that blood I see?"

"Oh, it's just a scrape," said Riley making light of his mother's concern. "I was horsing around back when we entered the park. I tripped and scrapped my knees. Nothin' to worry about, Mom," he said nonchalantly.

The remainder of the day was filled with fun and laughter. Each of the four kids ate everything they could convince their parents to buy leading up to Riley's father saying, "You kids have bottomless pits for stomachs."

Riley laughed. Then he startled everyone by saying. "Not a pit, Dad. More like Das Chute."

The vacation seemed to fly by and everyone was sad to see it come to an end. On the flight back to Chicago, Riley and William sat together. Riley's father sat on the aisle. Riley gave his cousin a nudge and said, "Look what I found."

William glanced down and looked at the strange colored stone his cousin had in the palm of his hand. "Where'd you find that?" he asked, taking the stone from Riley's hand and holding it up to the light coming through the plane's window.

The stone was almost the size of a baseball. "Cool, man. So, where did you find it?"

"You wouldn't believe me if I told you," said Riley. "Anyway, I think it's a real gold nugget."

"Yeah, right," replied William. He gave Riley's father a nudge and held out the nugget. "Hey, Unc, Riley said he found a gold nugget while we were in Disney World. Can you believe it?"

Riley's father examined the nugget and handed it across his nephew and gave it back to his son. Nice souvenir," he said. "Don't lose it. There might be some money in that rock." He smiled, closed his eyes and mumbled, "About as much money as the rocks in your head."

Chapter 13

Nothing more was said about Riley's gold nugget. The trip came to an end, and Riley and his sister were at home again. School started up after the break. Riley had placed his arrowhead and gold nugget in the night stand drawer in his bedroom where he kept all of his valuables; his baseball and football cards mainly. Then he forgot his two treasures from the Superstition Mountains. He didn't forget about Dutch, the Heart and Das Chute. Nor did he forget about Jesus and Guadalupe; and he couldn't forget about Blind Charlie. That is, until the following week when a new student joined his class at St. Pricilla's.

Riley's knees buckled when he saw the new student. "No way," he said aloud, as he headed for class on that Monday morning. The new student, he learned, had an older brother who was attending St. Patrick's High School. When he saw the new student again during the next passing period he didn't know what to say. He just stood and stared. "It can't be," he said, unable to turn down the volume attached to his words.

The new student heard him, turned and faced Riley.

Riley almost fainted, but managed to say, "Guadalupe, what are you doing here?"

The girl smiled and said, "I just moved here from Mexico." Her smile broadened showing perfect white teeth. "I'm here," she said, her eyes twinkling, "because this is where my parents want me to go to school." She walked up to him and asked: "How did you know my name?"

When Riley found his tongue he wanted to tell her that he knew her from the Superstition Mountains in Arizona and how he had helped her and her brother escape from the Apaches. "You have a brother, Jesus," he blurted out. "We met in the mountains by the Dutchman's mine."

"I don't know what you're talking about," she said, a look combining awe, fright and doubt reflecting back at Riley. "Are you playing some kind of mean trick on me?" she asked, as she turned and walked away from him without turning back.

"I'm not playing any trick," he said, as the girl disappeared into a classroom. "Honest, Guadalupe." He was crushed.

It didn't take Riley long to find out more about her. He stopped by the school's office and talked to the school's secretary, Mrs. Shea, a jovial woman who all of the students liked. "Is that new student's name, Guadalupe?" he asked.

"Are you asking because you know her?" Mrs. Shea asked. Then, her contagious smile popped up on her round, freckled face and she added, "Or do you want to know her?"

Riley felt his face catch on fire.

"She's really kind of cute, don't you think," said Mrs. Shea.

Riley's face burned brighter. He found that his tongue was stuck again.

"I shouldn't tell you this," said Mrs. Shea, "but her name is Guadalupe Pedraza and she and her older brother, Jesus moved here from Mexico. They're living with their grandmother."

"I'm going to prove to her that I know her," he said, after thanking Mrs. Shea and walking out of the office. Riley couldn't wait to get home and get to his nightstand drawer.

The school day seemed endless and finally when the bell rang Riley ran home. He snatched up the house key from the hiding place at the bottom of the faded black mail box attached to the brick wall next to the front door. Since both his parents worked, he didn't say a word. The door slammed behind him and he raced up the attic stairs to his room. "Darn it," he yelled, as he opened the drawer to his night stand. Both hands shuffled through the contents. "Darn it," he said again. "I know it's here." With both hands he pulled out the drawer and dumped the contents on his bed spread. "Where'd it go?" he asked, his hands picking through baseball and football cards, several stray marbles that had belonged to his father and several Oreo cookie wrappers. His hopes took a leap when he saw his arrowhead. He looked some more, his hands clamping down on his Boy Scout pocket knife. "Dutch's knife was twenty gazillion times bigger than this," he said, the knife dropping back into the drawer with an unceremonious thud. His stone, the gold nugget, the one that Dutch told him he could take if he wanted it, wasn't there. "I know I put it in here," he said to his empty bedroom. I know I did!" He searched and searched. No rock.

That night at the dinner table, Riley asked: "Did any of you see my gold nugget?" Frustrated, he sought out his mother. "Mom, did you happen to see my gold nugget?"

His sister made fun of him saying, "Oh, you and that silly chunk of worthless stone." She rolled her eyes. "Only losers save rocks," she continued, holding her thumb and index finger in the shape of an L and putting it up against her forehead. "Loser," she shouted out to him.

"Oh, Elsa, stop with your nonsense," Riley's mother said.

"We don't talk like that in this house." She shook her head at her daughter and then looked at Riley. "Oh, that precious rock of yours is probably in the pocket of your favorite hiking shorts; the ones you wore on vacation to Disney World."

"Yeah, that's it," he said, jumping up from the table and shouting, "My shorts!" He was about to head for the basement stairs where the dirty laundry was piled awaiting wash day when he felt his father's hand on his arm.

"Whoa, Lone Ranger," his father ordered. "Slow down. I took your golden rock."

"Why'd you do that, Dad?" he asked.

Riley's father sat back in his chair. "I talked to your grand-father and he wanted to see it so I mailed it out to Arizona."

"You mailed it back to Arizona?" asked Riley sounding upset. "Didn't anyone ask me if they could take my stuff and send it away? Gee whiz. That really stinks!"

"Oh, calm down, Grizzly Adams Junior," his father said. "You sound just like your grandfather. Too bad you're not a junior instead of me."

"Gee, Dad, I wish you would've asked me first. I really need that rock," he said. He didn't tell his father that he wanted to show it to the new girl in his class in hopes that she might remember that they had met before.

"Your grandfather had called here asking about our trip to Disney World and how we liked it," he said, retelling the conversation that Riley knew nothing about. "During the course of talking to your Grandpa Rocky, I told him about your roller coaster ride and you finding this golden rock of yours. He wanted to see it so, I sent it to him."

"When will I get it back?" asked Riley, his question

sounding snippy.

"You'll get it back when your grandfather sends it back," his father snapped. "Now get off your high horse, masked man and sit down and finish your dinner. I ain't workin' so you can waste food."

Riley plopped down in his chair with a thud. He felt his world collapsing around him and all he could think of was the black haired Guadalupe.

"Relax," his father said to him. "Personally, I think your grandfather has lost his marbles. One of those marbles is likely that rock of yours."

"But why did Grandpa want to see my rock?"

"Your grandfather said something about wanting to have it assayed or something like that. He wanted to check and see if it had any value. Personally, I think your grandfather has been spending too much time wandering in those silly Arizona Mountains. The man's fried his old brain in that sunshine and heat." His father let out a laugh and looked at Riley's mother. "But, it's a dry heat, ain't it?"

That same evening as the family was getting ready for bed Riley's father came into his room and sat down on his bed. He seemed way too serious. "I talked to your grandfather tonight after your little temper tantrum."

"I'm sorry, Dad," Riley said sheepishly.

"Don't worry about it," his father said. He looked at his son. "Your grandfather took your so-called golden rock into some place to have it checked out to see what it was made of." His father pursed his lips then licked them.

Riley saw his father's eyebrows raise as his tongue continued to slide back and forth across his lips. "Did you ever hear the expression, fool's gold?" his father asked, his eyebrows still up and arched.

"Grandpa told me about it once."

"You know that a rock the size of the one you said you found up on those Superstition Mountains would be worth a lot of money if it were indeed real gold."

Riley shrugged and said, "I guess."

"I guess too," his father said as he got up off the bed and stood facing his son. "Riley, I don't know where you found that thing or how you even got your hands on it, but, Son, your grandfather told me that you didn't find any fool's gold."

Riley wasn't sure as to what his father had just said to him. He didn't say a word. Just as he was about to speak, his mother came into the room. She looked like she had been crying. Elsa followed her mother into the room and quickly put her thumb and forefinger L to her forehead.

His father laughed. Riley didn't. He had a vivid memory of Dutch telling him it was okay to take a rock from the mine. He thought he remembered the Dutchman saying to him something about something to remember me by."

"Thank you, Dutch, Sir," he remembered, saying to the old man as they stood in the center of the Heart. He had shown the strange looking rock to his new friends, Jesus and Guadalupe. Neither of them had called him a loser. There was no laughter or tears, only a keen interest. A rock like that was what their families had been digging in the mines for. If it was one thing Riley knew, his experiences with Dutch were real. So was his saving Blind Charlie from the Apache band. He didn't care if no one else believed him. He wasn't a loser and his special rock wasn't for fools.

His father looked at him and said, "Son, I don't know where you found that rock, but your grandfather had it analyzed and valued. You must have found it when we were hiking with your grandfather in the Superstitions." His father paused and looked at Riley then he looked at Riley's mother. He let out a slow exhale. "Elsa, get that hand off your forehead and stop acting silly." He looked back at Riley. "Son, you're no fool and neither is your rock. Your grandfather wanted me to tell you he's going to put it in his safety deposit box in the bank. The thing is real gold and worth a lot of money."

Riley wasn't surprised. "I knew it was real," he said, a nonchalance in his voice. "Dutch told me it was."

Title: Where Have All the Go-Go's Gone?

Part I

- Author: Richard Baran
- Publisher: TotalRecall Publications, Inc.
- Hard Cover, ISBN: 9781590952399
- Paperback, ISBN: 9781590952405
- Ebook, Nook, Kindle, ISBN: 9781590952412
- Number of pages: 304
- Publication Date: 2015

Bo Pepperwall's intelligence dwarfed Mensa's parameters. He was perceived as strange thereby resulting in his being ridiculed by many, shunned by most and being called, Bo the Schmoe by all. Then he faced a dilemma. He had to choose between money (which he never had) and morals (which he also lacked). Should he weasel a part of his recently widowed sister's inheritance for a business venture or should he turn in the killer of her husband, his despicable brother-in-law? He chooses both. Bo opens La Tinkerbelle's a Go-Go, a 1960's retro discotheque in an abandoned factory building in a Chicago slum using a theme from the legend of Peter Pan. Surrounding himself with bizarre employees (each having a unique vision of reality) who put fun into dysfunctional, his dream nearly goes bust. Then a Chicago gossip columnist prints a story that has customers lined up and Bo collides with his dilemma. The collision buries him in money and public adulation. Success, however, can't cover his moral guilt in the surprise ending to this murder mystery farce that is more farce than mystery.

Title: When Will They Ever Learn?

Part II Where Have All the Go-Go's Gone?

- Author: Richard Baran
- Publisher: TotalRecall Publications, Inc.
- Hard Cover, ISBN: 9781590952429
- Paperback, ISBN: 9781590952436
- Ebook, Nook, Kindle, ISBN: 9781590952443
- Number of pages: 220
- Publication Date: 2015

Bo Pepperwall, a card carrying member of Mensa, dreamer, conniver and ridiculed lifelong loser opens *La Tinkerbelle's a Go-Go*. A 1960's retro discotheque located in a Chicago slum, he uses a theme from the legend of Peter Pan that includes a scantily clad Tinker Bell. He finances his business by weaseling part of his sister's inheritance away from her. He also witnesses the murder of his despicable brother-in-law, the mayor of Glen Forest on the Watercourse, a prestigious Chicago North Shore community. Bo, however, remains a loser and his garish disco faces bankruptcy until an article by a Chicago gossip columnist turns it into a bonanza. That same day, Tinker Bell's outraged mother accidentally sets fire to La Tinkerbelle's and destroys the booming business. Bo and his employees—along with two black cats named Heckle and Jeckle—end up in court charged with violations of the Mann Act; contributing to the delinquency of minors; ignoring EPA laws; cruelty to animals and presenting lewd and indecent performances. Bo turns in the killer and the court finds him innocent of the criminal charges in the surprise ending to this murder mystery zany comedy.

Title: The Jacket

- Author: Richard Baran
- Publisher: TotalRecall Publications, Inc.
- Hard Cover ISBN: 9781590955659
- Paperback, ISBN: 9781590955666
- Ebook, Nook, Kindle, ISBN: 9781590955673
- Number of pages: 352
- Publication Date: 2013

Tidge Mackiewicz, new patriarch of his family, received several orders from his dying father, Kid Scream. One order stated that Tidge should quit believing in Santa Claus and stop acting like every day was Christmas. Tidge should also abandon his belief that the Luftwaffe shot down Santa Claus on Christmas Eve in 1944 and Santa survived.